"Now, ARE YOU GOING TO KISS IT AND MAKE IT BETTER?" Trevor asked.

Jana dropped the cloth she'd used to clean his wound. "Kiss it?"

"My mother always kissed the ouchie and made it better," he teased.

"I am not your mother."

"No, you're not." He grinned suggestively. "So a kiss on the lips will do."

She stepped away from him. "I don't think so."

"I think you owe it to me," he said, moving closer.

"You already got your kiss in that cave you took me to."

"That was to stop you from getting all hysterical on me."

"It was still a kiss," she said, backing herself against the wall. Wide-eyed, she looked around for a way to escape.

He closed the space between them, blocking all exits. "Afraid to kiss me?"

"Of course not." She lifted her chin boldly, looking him straight in the eyes. "What's there to be afraid of?"

He smiled, weaving his fingers through her hair. "Exactly. . . ."

WHAT ARE *LOVESWEPT* ROMANCES?

They are stories of true romance and touching emotion. We believe those two very important ingredients are constants in our highly sensual and very believable stories in the LOVE-SWEPT line. Our goal is to give you, the reader, stories of consistently high quality that may sometimes make you laugh, sometimes make you cry, but are always fresh and creative and contain many delightful surprises within their pages.

Most romance fans read an enormous number of books. Those they truly love, they keep. Others may be traded with friends and soon forgotten. We hope that each LOVESWEPT romance will be a treasure—a "keeper." We will always try to publish

LOVE STORIES YOU'LL NEVER FORGET
BY AUTHORS YOU'LL ALWAYS REMEMBER

The Editors

SHELTER
FROM THE
STORM

MARIS
SOULE

BANTAM BOOKS
NEW YORK · TORONTO · LONDON · SYDNEY · AUCKLAND

SHELTER FROM THE STORM
A Bantam Book / November 1997

ISBN 0-553-44595-2

Published simultaneously in the United States and Canada

Bantam Books are published by Bantam Books, a division of Bantam Dou-
bleday Dell Publishing Group, Inc. Its trademark, consisting of the words
"Bantam Books" and the portrayal of a rooster, is Registered in U.S.
Patent and Trademark Office and in other countries. Marca Registrada.
Bantam Books, 1540 Broadway, New York, New York 10036.

PRINTED IN THE UNITED STATES OF AMERICA
OPM   10 9 8 7 6 5 4 3 2 1

My thanks to Gil Collver for his help. Without him, I never could have hijacked a plane. And thank you, Tanya, for answering my questions about the Bahamas.

PROLOGUE

"PASSWORD," the monitor screen flashed.

Jana Jenkins typed in her password, hit the enter key, and waited for the menu to come up. Her stepbrother leaned closer.

"Is that all you have to do?" he asked. "Just type in that one password and you're into everything?"

"Everything I have clearance for," she answered. Which was most of the accounts in the bank. She clicked the mouse on the icon for the program Jeff had promised to help her master in one easy lesson.

"Seems as if they should have tighter security than that." He looked around the lobby.

Jana also looked up. The clock said ten minutes to four, and only a few customers waited for tellers, normal for a Thursday afternoon in July. Friday was when the big rush came, and she worried about security and robberies.

"Trust me, Jeff, if someone else got this password—

and I don't see how they could—one suspicious transaction would trigger an alert. I told you about making that one large transfer for Senor Alvarez last month and how security was at my desk in minutes, checking to make sure—"

Her monitor screen went blank.

"Oh darn, I'm sorry." Jeff knelt at her feet, reached under her desk, and replugged her computer. "I caught the cord with my foot."

"I thought I had that back far enough." Jana waited for her computer to reboot. "So where do I have to take you to dinner to pay for this computer lesson?"

"How's the Radisson Hotel downtown Detroit sound?"

"Expensive." She again typed in her password.

"Carl's Chop House?"

Jana didn't have a chance to answer. At that moment the front doors banged open, and four men wearing ski masks burst into the bank, waving handguns and semiautomatics. A teller screamed, and out of the corner of her eye, Jana saw Craig Morrison, the bank manager, rise from his chair behind the desk in his office.

The four men shouted orders, and Jana sat and watched the people in the front of the bank move in response. It all seemed like a movie, her mind not really comprehending what was happening. One of the men strode toward her, only his dark eyes showing, everything else about his face hidden. He yelled for her to lie face down on the floor. She didn't move. She couldn't move.

"Better do as he says," Jeff said. His voice sounded

shaky, but his hand on her elbow was steady. He eased her out of her chair and down onto her knees.

Her skirt hiked up, and she tried to pull it lower. "I says down, lady," the hooded robber ordered, and kicked at her with the edge of his boot, sending her sprawling to her side.

"You don't have to hurt her!" her stepbrother yelled, rising to his feet to face the man.

She admired Jeff for his courage, but cringed, waiting for the robber's response. From her position on the floor, she watched the robber step forward and her stepbrother move back. "You know everything, man?" the robber asked, glaring at Jeff.

"I know what I need to know," Jeff said boldly.

"That's good, man. Very good for you." The robber chuckled. " 'Cause now, we gonna take you with us."

"You can't!" Jana started to get up.

From behind her, a boot against her back forced her onto the floor again, and another voice spoke up. "We're ready if you are."

Her hair was across her eyes, and she could see only part of what was happening. The dark-eyed robber with the Jamaican-sounding voice was pointing a gun at her stepbrother's back and making him walk toward the door. "Jeff!" she cried out, lifting her head.

Again she was shoved down.

Only when her brother and the robber were out of the bank did the other three men back out, shouting warnings and threats until they disappeared through the doorway.

The clock on the wall showed exactly four o'clock.

ONE

The battered radio on the shelf behind the counter crackled with static as the local weather forecaster gave Hurricane Ned's most recent position in the Atlantic. Trevor Fox cursed under his breath. Good old Hurricane Ned had cost him a charter that morning. The couple had backed out, deciding to leave Florida before the hurricane hit. Trevor had told them there was little danger, that most of the hurricanes that formed in the Atlantic dissipated or veered north before reaching Vero Beach, but it hadn't helped. Now he had a plane all fueled up and no charter. One more day without any income and another payment due on the Navajo.

As he brooded over a cup of coffee, he watched a blue Ford Escort pull into the parking lot next to his office. It looked like a rental car. The brunette who got out was slender and short, her dark hair waving softly past her shoulders. She looked to be in her late twenties or early thirties, though the oversized dark glasses covering her eyes and most of the upper half of her face kept him from really telling.

Her nose was small and delicately shaped, and her mouth was slightly pouty, her lips colored a deep rose. The blue blouse she wore had a silky sheen and was unbuttoned nearly to her waist. The open neckline led his gaze to a deep cleavage and the definite curve of her breasts. There was nothing subtle about what she was advertising, though her loose fitting tan slacks didn't show off her figure as well as a pair of jeans or shorts might have.

She also wore open-toed high-heeled sandals and carried a leather handbag half her size. He watched her walk toward his door, the quickening of his heartbeat surprising him. After thirty-two years of being dumped on by women, he considered himself immune to their charms. Evidently he still had a weakness for the opposite sex. At least for dark-haired females with pouty lips.

She smiled as she entered his office, and he knew he was a goner. *I'm yours*, he thought, and silently laughed at the idea. He could offer himself to her, but considering the poor shape of his bank account and his tarnished reputation, he doubted she'd be a taker. At best he could hope she wanted to charter his plane.

"Mr. Fox? Trevor Fox?" she asked, her soft, sweet voice matching the scent of flowery perfume that greeted him as she neared.

"You got him," he said, straightening behind the counter and pushing his coffee cup to the side. "What can I do for you?"

She slipped off the dark glasses, giving him a good

look at her eyes. He'd expected brown and was surprised to find they were a muted green with flecks of gold. "I need you," she said.

And I need you, baby, he thought. Maybe for just a few hours, but he was sure the experience would be one he'd never forget. What he said aloud relayed none of his emotions. "Are you looking for a charter or a flying lesson?"

"A charter," she said, and opened her handbag to pull out a letter-sized envelope about an inch thick. "I'm Jan . . . ah . . . Janice Jones, and I'm with a movie studio. It's . . . ah—ah private studio. My job is to check out suitable locations for filming." She glanced out the window facing the airport. His plane sat on the tarmac, ready for the charter that had canceled.

Looking back at him, she took in a breath and again smiled. "We have a couple scenes for a movie coming up that need to be shot along the Florida coast. Somewhere between here and the Marathon Key. What I would like is for you to fly me down there and back. Today."

"Today?" It was short notice and already nine o'clock.

She glanced back out the window, then up at the sky. Gray clouds blocked the sun, though visibility was still good. "I understand a storm's headed this way. I need to get this done right now. Time is of the essence."

"You just want to fly down the coast and back?"

"Basically." She didn't look at him but opened the envelope, pulling out a wad of bills. "I can pay you well."

He stared at the money. It had been a long time since

he'd seen that many hundred dollar bills. Most of the people who came through his door paid with plastic.

"There are some stipulations," she continued.

He lifted his eyebrows, wondering just what those stipulations would be. One thing he didn't need was anything illegal. The Drug Enforcement Agency already had him under surveillance. It seemed one mistake branded a man for life.

"Nothing too difficult, really." She leaned forward a little, the neckline of her blouse gaping open and giving him a good view of creamy white flesh.

"What I need," she said, her tone almost sultry, "is to take some pictures. Which means you're going to have to fly fairly low. Will that be a problem?"

"No." His Piper Navajo could be navigated under instrument flight rules or visual flight rules. Despite the clouds, visibility was good beyond three miles. He could fly along the coast under the visual flight rules with no problems.

"And you can carry enough fuel to go six to eight hundred miles?"

"Easily."

"Good." Again she smiled. Sweetly. Alluringly. "So what do you say?"

Considering his financial situation, the answer was easy. "Can you be ready in an hour?"

That hour seemed like an eternity to Jana. Away from the airport, she changed from her high-heeled sandals to the sneakers she knew she'd need later, checked the 9 mm semiautomatic pistol she'd been practicing with for the last two weeks, and slung around her neck the 35 mm camera she needed to make her story convincing.

Playing the seductress and walking around with her blouse half unbuttoned had not been easy, but she had to admit, Trevor Fox had spent more time looking at her chest than at her eyes and had agreed to her arrangement a lot more easily than she'd expected. Uncle Nicky knew what he was talking about. She just hoped everything else he'd told her was correct. She also hoped she could go through with this.

If she'd had a choice, she wouldn't have involved anyone else. But she didn't have a choice. Her stepbrother's life and her own depended on the next few hours. Besides, from what Uncle Nicky had told her, Trevor Fox was no innocent. He was a drug smuggler and deserved anything that might happen to him.

She returned to the office of Fox Charters exactly one hour after she'd left. Trevor looked the same as when she'd left. He was wearing a blue-and-white check oxford shirt, tan chinos, and brown leather boots. He nodded when she entered, picked up a small flight bag and a clipboard, and motioned for her to precede him out the side door to the plane.

"For some reason, I expected more cameras," he said, glancing at the one hanging around her neck, the strap pressed tight against her breasts.

Once again, his gaze stayed on her breasts longer than necessary. She arched her back, sticking out her chest. She could almost hear Uncle Nicky saying, *Play up your sex appeal. If he's thinking of ways to get you into the sack, he won't suspect a thing.* She didn't need Trevor Fox questioning her story.

"I have what I need," she said, and hoped that was true.

"You been doing this long?" he asked.

"No." Everything in the last two months of her life had been a new experience. She gave him another smile and dropped her voice to what she trusted was a sexy whisper. "I'm really hoping you'll help me with this. I'm going to be relying on you."

She saw his shoulders straighten, his male ego taking over. "I'll do what I can," he said.

He helped her into the plane, then followed her into the cramped space, indicating a seat she might take. She looked back at him. "Do you mind if I sit up front, next to you? I know it's probably not usually done, but I'm fascinated by airplanes, and I actually think I'll get a better view of where we're going and what's below from up there. Also, it will be easier to talk to you. Easier to ask you questions."

"Sure. No problem." He chuckled and slipped into his seat after taking care of his flight bag. "Most of the time I'm asked to pull the curtain." He indicated the draped cloth pushed back behind his seat. "I think seeing all of the dials and gauges up here makes them nervous. That or they don't want me to know what's going on back there."

He started to slip on the headphones. Again she stopped him, this time placing a hand on his arm. "If you put those on, I won't be able to hear what the tower tells you, will I?"

He hesitated. "No."

"I'd love to hear what a pilot says to the tower, and what the tower tells a pilot. You see it in movies, but to be here . . ." She laughed, glancing down as if embarrassed. "You probably think I'm silly."

"No." He reached across her, grabbing another headset by her side. "You could use these. Actually, it would make conversation easier."

"I . . ." She paused, giving him the coy smile she'd been practicing. "You really are going to think I'm trying to make things difficult, but I just can't stand to have anything pressed against my head like that. I think it goes back to an accident I had as a child when I had earphones on."

For a moment he seemed undecided, and Jana held her breath, then he shrugged, put the extra headset back in place, and clipped his own headset into its holder. Picking up a hand microphone, he pointed to perforated ovals above her head. "Those are the speakers. You'll be able to hear everything that's said."

She smiled appreciatively and let out a sigh of relief as he checked in and requested a visual departure. Switches were turned on, the engines started, and controls checked. She watched him work, impressed with his ease and self-assurance. Gazing at his profile, she decided he was much better looking than the picture Uncle Nicky had shown her. Then again, Trevor Fox had only been sixteen in that picture, lanky and pimple-faced, his sandy blond hair too long, and his boyish immaturity clear to see.

Life had not been easy for Trevor from what Uncle

Nicky had told her. Certainly not as easy as when he'd spent his summers on Conch Island with his father. That was before he joined the marines . . . before he got into trouble.

In the years since that picture had been taken, the pimples had disappeared, the lanky frame had filled out, and his hair was much shorter, a few gray strands now scattered among the blond. She was seated next to a man hard with experience and tainted by scandal. She found it ironic. A few months earlier, she would have avoided someone like him. Now she was seeking him out. Even more ironic, she actually found him appealing.

Only when he was certain all was in order and the tower gave him the okay did he taxi toward the runway. Once again Jana held her breath as the engines roared. Her heart was in her throat, her stomach in knots, but she knew it wasn't simply the idea of flying that had her so tense. This was it. The beginning that she hoped would bring an end to the nightmare she'd been living for the last two months. From the day those robbers had burst into her bank, her life had been a living hell.

"Ready?" Trevor asked.

She swallowed hard. "Ready."

Jana said nothing more until the plane was in the air. The steady drone of the engines soothed some of the tension away, but the noise also made hearing difficult. It would have been easier to use the headsets, but Uncle Nicky had warned her not to. "There's a button on the controls," he'd said. "All the guy would have to do is push it—you probably wouldn't even see him do it—and everyone back at the control tower might hear every word you were saying. They'd have you on the ground before you could count to ten."

She couldn't let that happen.

The voice coming through the speakers confirmed that they were on radar. Looking out the side window, she searched for the landmarks she had to find. Each would signal her next move.

"You just let me know when you want to take a picture," Trevor yelled above the engine noise, and she nodded, too dry-mouthed to answer.

Air turbulence jostled the plane, adding to the queasiness in her stomach. She prayed she didn't really get sick, but was pleased when Trevor reported the turbulence over the radio. It would make the story he was going to tell later more believable. "How far to Witham?" she asked.

He glanced her way, his expression indicating his surprise at the mention of the airport. "About twenty-five nautical miles, I'd say."

"Good." She reached into her handbag, her fingers wrapping around the handle of the 9 mm pistol nestled next to her billfold. The moment was getting close. Timing would be everything.

She waited until he was looking straight ahead before she slipped the gun from her bag. Turning slightly in her seat, she aimed it at him. "I want you to call the tower and tell them there's been a change in your flight plan, that your passenger isn't feeling well, that I'm sick, and you're going to have to make an emergency landing at Witham."

"You're what?" He looked at her, frowning his lack of

understanding. She moved her hand, and he noticed the gun. "What the—?"

"Don't think I won't use it," she said, surprised by how calm she sounded. "I know enough about flying to put this plane down by myself."

"But—" His gaze switched from the gun to her face. "I don't get it. You said . . . You—"

"There's nothing to get. Just relay the message I gave you."

She kept the pistol aimed toward his middle and prayed he would do as she'd asked. Whether she could actually pull the trigger was not something she wanted to find out. "Tell them you have a sick passenger and are going to have to land at Witham. Say exactly that and nothing more. Whatever you do, don't try anything funny."

He relayed the message basically as she'd given it. Jana hoped the person on the other end didn't notice the hesitancy in Trevor's voice. Once he'd gotten the okay to descend, she took the mike from his hand.

"Now," she went on, "I want you to go down as if we were going to land at Witham."

"As if—"

She didn't let him finish. "Just do it."

"I don't know what you think you're doing." He glanced at the gun again.

"Do it," she repeated.

She watched the needle on the gauge as they descended. Ahead of them she could see the airport, just as Uncle Nicky had said she would. She handed the mike back to Trevor. "Now tell them you have the airport in sight."

He did as ordered, and got the response she'd hoped for. "Okay, radar canceled," came the message. "Frequency change approved. Squawk VFR."

She watched as Trevor reached toward the transponder. A seven came up, and her stomach tightened. "Don't go through 7500," she warned. "Or 7700. Put in 1200." She knew the first two numbers were the codes for a hijack and an emergency. Either would alert the tower monitoring them that there was trouble.

He glanced her way, frowned, and dialed in 1200. She watched the needle drop to 500 feet and reached forward. With the turn of a knob, she turned off the transponder.

"I take it you do know how to fly one of these," he said, glancing at her again. "Why did you bother with me? Why didn't you just take my plane?"

"I have my reasons." She kept an eye on the needle. The plane continued to descend.

"What's at Witham?"

"Nothing." She gauged the distance and decided they were on target. "Now I want you to take a heading of 120, and descend to 200 feet as soon as we clear land."

"120?" he repeated, not moving his hands from the controls.

"Dial XAY into your GPS." She tapped the face of the instrument for the global positioning system used by most planes and ships.

"XAY?" He frowned. "That's the old abandoned airstrip on Conch Island."

"Exactly." Again, she nodded toward the GPS. "And I suggest you get it dialed in unless you want to depend on visual to find that island."

He dialed in the code letters and looked at her. "Are you going to tell me what this is about, or am I just flying blind?"

"It's about mistakes and being at the wrong place at the wrong time. It's about people not believing you."

Trevor could understand mistakes in judgment and people not believing the truth. What he didn't understand was what had happened to make a pretty brunette desperate enough to hijack a plane. And why his plane?

"You're not going to get away with this," he said.

She shrugged.

"Have you ever been to Conch Island?"

"No."

Her voice sounded shaky, and he noticed the barrel of the gun wasn't steady. Under other circumstances, he could probably disarm her quite easily, but in a plane flying over water, the idea would be foolish, if not deadly. His best bet was to wait and see where this led.

"I used to spend my summers on Conch Island," he said. "It's fifteen square miles of nothing but boggy marshes, trees, and rocks. Other than the village near the airstrip, the place is uninhabitable. It doesn't even have a really good beach."

"Your father lived there."

He was surprised that she knew that. "My father was a crazy recluse."

"From the people I talked to, he was a pretty good artist."

Trevor shrugged. "Some people liked his work."

"I saw the painting in your office. I liked it. I also know another man who has one of your father's paintings. He thought a lot of your father."

"Oh, yeah? And what's this man's name?"

"Nicholas Scarlotti."

Trevor looked at her, surprised that the name could still send a chill down his spine. Nick the Terminator wasn't a man many admitted knowing. Trevor's acquaintance with him was limited to one summer, the year he'd turned sixteen. He'd never understood his father's friendship with a known Mafia hit man, and wouldn't have expected the woman seated next to him to know Nicholas Scarlotti. Then again, he hadn't expected a lot of things from her. Once more, he'd been duped by a pretty face. "This is about drugs, isn't it?"

"No, though I'm sure you're accustomed to flying drug dealers around."

"I've never flown—" The lift of her eyebrows stopped him. "Well, except that once, and believe me, I didn't know."

"Ah yes, you guys are always innocent, aren't you? Uncle Nicky said if I showed you that wad of bills, you'd go along with anything I said. And boy, was he right. You took one look at that money and everything was set."

Trevor grumbled, not liking her description of his nature or what he'd heard. "Nicholas Scarlotti is your uncle?"

"No. We're not related."

"But you called him uncle?"

"You know how it is when you're little. Older people

become Aunt This and Uncle That. I hadn't seen Nicholas Scarlotti for over seventeen years, but I've always thought of him as 'Uncle Nicky.'"

"Seventeen years." Trevor took a guess. "You were what? Nine, ten years old then?"

"Eleven."

That made her twenty-eight, beautiful, and obviously dangerous. "So if it's not drugs, why are you hijacking my plane?"

She hesitated a moment, then answered. "Actually I'm surprised you didn't recognize me. My picture's been in the paper quite a bit lately. My name isn't Jones, it's Jenkins. Jana Jenkins."

The name meant nothing to him. "So?"

"So . . . Two months ago the bank where I worked was robbed and my stepbrother was taken hostage. It was headline news in the Detroit area, especially when the police accused me of being in on the robbery."

"I vaguely remember something about a bank robbery in Detroit." He tried to recall what he'd read. "I'm afraid I didn't pay much attention to it, though." He'd had other things on his mind. Like bills that needed paying.

She glanced at his control panel, then back at him. "Are we nearing the Air Defense Intercept Zone?"

"Yeah."

"I think you'd better drop to one hundred feet so you're under radar."

She knew the steps necessary to pull off this hijacking, including the fact that there was a section of air space over the water where an aircraft needed to identify itself for the sake of national security and that the only way to avoid detection in this zone was to fly below radar. He had to admit, it would be difficult explaining why he was flying toward the Bahamas without an international flight plan. No one would believe he'd been hijacked by this pint-sized beauty. He still couldn't believe it himself.

He took the Piper down to one hundred feet.

The water was choppy beneath them, a sign that they were flying toward the turbulence of Hurricane Ned. It seemed he was flying with danger, and flying into it. "What does Conch Island have to do with a robbery in Detroit?"

"Uncle Nicky heard my stepbrother's there."

"So you're going to join him? Hide out on the island?" It wouldn't be the first time thieves had used Conch as a hideaway. Scarlotti was a prime example.

"Join the robbers? No. I'm going to rescue my stepbrother."

"Yeah, sure."

"I am. Don't you understand? My stepbrother's being held hostage."

"By how many men?"

"I'm not sure. There were four in the robbery."

He laughed. "So you're going to fly in there, do battle with four robbers, and rescue your stepbrother. Who do you think you are, John Wayne?"

"I can do it."

He looked at her, then at the gun she held. "And were those robbers armed?"

"Yes."

She licked her lips, and he found his gaze drawn to her mouth. Under other circumstances, he'd be plotting ways to steal a kiss. Under these circumstances, he knew he had to talk her out of her foolish plan. "Why not just tell the authorities where these robbers are and let them rescue your stepbrother and arrest these men?"

"Because . . ." She looked away from him. "There's a little bit more of a problem."

He had a feeling there was a lot more of a problem. "Such as?"

"Well . . . I can't just go to the police because I sort of left Michigan when I wasn't supposed to. If I go to them, I don't think they'd listen to anything I said . . . or if they did, it might be too late by then. Uncle Nicky said he didn't think these men would stay on Conch long."

Trevor wasn't sure why they were there at all. "If you're innocent, why do the police want you?"

"Because not only did the robbers take my stepbrother as a hostage, but somehow, in the hour after the robbery, they managed to break into the bank's computer system, using my password, and transferred a lot of money out before anyone realized what was happening."

"And how did they get your password?"

She shook her head. "That's the problem; I don't know."

"From your stepbrother?"

"He didn't know it. In fact, I'd just changed my password that morning. We do that on a regular basis. No one should have known it."

"No one but you." Trevor now understood why she was a suspect.

"Everyone thinks I'm involved. The police, the FBI, and Senor Alvarez.

"And who is Senor Alvarez?"

"A South American investor I've been working with. Most of the money that was transferred was his." She grimaced and leaned slightly toward him. "Don't you see? If I can get my stepbrother back, he can explain what happened. He knows computers backward and forward. He has his own computer business. That's why he was there that day, to help me with a new program. I'm sure he could tell Senor Alvarez and the others how those men did it. Maybe he could even tell us where they transferred the money."

"I assume then that you're planning on my not only flying you to Conch but flying the two of you back?"

She nodded.

"And what's to guarantee I'll cooperate?"

She waved the gun. "This and the fact that you'll be paid for your efforts. You saw the money in that envelope. It's all yours if you help me."

"No matter what you think about me, I'm not stupid. Money isn't going to help if I'm arrested for aiding and abetting a criminal." He'd learned that the hard way in the marines. Back then he'd managed to get off with just a dishonorable discharge. He had a feeling he wouldn't be as lucky this time.

"You won't be arrested. Once we rescue my stepbrother, you'll be a hero."

"*If* you rescue your stepbrother."

"Uncle Nicky said we have a fifty-fifty chance of suc-ceeding."

She was involving him, and fifty-fifty didn't sound that good to him. "And if 'we' don't succeed?"

"We've got to. There's no other way."

The look in her green eyes was a combination of fear and determination, and with a gun in her hand, she was potentially lethal. He knew he was being a sucker again because for some reason, he wanted to help her.

TWO

The first time the plane jerked, Jana thought Trevor was doing it. She was ready for him to try something like that. "Never let your guard down," Uncle Nicky had warned her. She wasn't.

From the moment she'd pulled the gun on Trevor, she'd been expecting him to try to disarm her. Making the plane jerk and bounce would be a good way to get her off balance. On the other hand, a struggle in the cockpit wouldn't be wise. Below them was nothing but open water, and though they'd climbed back to an altitude of two hundred feet after they'd passed through the Air Defense Intercept Zone, two hundred feet was close enough to see the roiling swells and choppy waves below. One mistake could put them into those foamy whitecaps.

The plane bounced again, and she realized Trevor hadn't done it. Air turbulence had. The sky had become a gray blanket, heavy with the rain it had yet to let loose. They were flying into Hurricane Ned.

The plane jerked.

"You picked a helluva day to hijack a plane," Trevor grumbled, his words strained and his knuckles white from clutching the control yoke.

"I thought you said the hurricane would go out to sea or dissipate," she shouted above the wind and engine noise.

"That was when I thought we'd be flying south, along the coastline of Florida," he yelled back. "In case you haven't been paying attention, *we* are flying out to sea. That means we're flying directly into the damn thing."

She glanced at the control panel, then at her watch. "Shouldn't we be almost there?"

"Do you see it?"

Jana strained to see any signs of land. For the last two weeks, she'd been memorizing aeronautical charts. With seven hundred islands and two thousand cays—which she'd learned were pronounced "keys"—making up the Commonwealth of the Bahamas, it would be all too easy to land in the wrong spot, all too easy to make a mistake and miss finding her stepbrother. She knew the few islands they had passed over were not Conch Island. Conch wasn't much bigger than many of the cays and had gotten its name because it was shaped like a conch shell. According to her calculations, it should be straight ahead and coming into view.

Should be . . .

"You haven't gone off course, have you?" she asked.

"If you'd let me switch on the transponder, we could check."

He started to reach for it. She reacted immediately. "Don't touch that."

Another jerk of the plane rocked her in her seat, the muzzle of her pistol bobbing. She saw him glance at it and steeled herself, ready for him to grab for the gun. To her relief, his hand went back to the controls, and he looked forward again.

"There," he said, and nodded his head. "Straight ahead."

It took her a moment to see where water turned to land. The shoreline ahead of them was not a beckoning beach but a ragged outline of elevated limestone being beaten by angry waves. Although Cat Island boasted the highest elevation in the Bahamas, its loftiest peak reaching 204 feet above sea level, Jana knew that Conch Island had many spots nearly that high.

Trevor adjusted the plane's altitude, and the knot in her stomach twisted tighter. She'd accomplished the first step of her plan. They were there. Now she had to think of the next step—finding Jeff.

"I've got to let them know we're landing," Trevor said. "They get funny if you just drop in."

Jana hesitated. Uncle Nicky hadn't said anything about contacting the airport when they landed. He'd simply said it was an abandoned airstrip, and they wouldn't have any problems. But then, it had been a long time since Nicholas Scarlotti had lived on Conch Island. Maybe he wasn't up-to-date on that point.

Finally she made a decision. "Tell them we got off course. Use the excuse that I'm ill. Tell them we won't be here long."

"Sure." Trevor reached over and switched on the transponder. She didn't stop him this time, and he mentally debated how to word a message.

He hoped Charlie Walker was listening. The old man had a collection of CBs, transmitters, and receivers, but he didn't always turn them on, and it was well known on Conch Island that after five in the afternoon Charlie's consumption of the local brew picked up to a point where his comprehension of anything he heard dropped dramatically. Since it was before five, Trevor figured he might have a chance. And even if Charlie didn't hear him, someone at one of the other Out Islands should. The fact that he'd suddenly appeared out of nowhere should cause a stir and get this landing reported to the proper authorities.

"Navajo 8-0-3-4," he shouted into the mike. "Requesting landing instructions."

His response was static.

He tried the message two more times, each time with the same results. Whether Charlie or anyone else was listening didn't seem to matter. The storm was playing its part in this drama, tearing up the air waves. Trevor switched off the transponder.

He'd lied about anyone caring if they landed. The airport at Conch wasn't an Airport of Entry. There would be no immigration personnel around to question a plane landing unexpectedly. Actually the landing strip on Conch Island couldn't be classified as an airport at all.

Back in the 80s, when drug running was at its height in the Bahamas, the airstrip had mysteriously appeared, just as Nicholas Scarlotti had mysteriously appeared.

There was never a hangar. No terminal. Here a pilot found nothing more than fuel pumps—which sometimes had fuel—and a set of tools that might get you by if you needed minor repairs.

The summer he'd turned sixteen, planes had landed and taken off regularly. The next summer, Scarlotti and his men were gone, and so were the planes. After that, only an occasional tourist landed there. More often than not, they were lost.

Charlie had taken over guardianship of the airstrip. When he did respond to a pilot, he generally guided the plane away from the island. The Bahamas Tourist Board might have the welcome mat out, but the inhabitants of Conch Island liked their isolation. Tourism was openly discouraged. In the last twenty years the population had barely changed, the few additions from births balanced by the passing of some of the older generation and some of the younger generation leaving to find more excitement in Nassau or Freeport.

Most of the locals were descendants of early Bermudian immigrants, slaves, and pirates. Only rarely was a newcomer—especially a white man—welcomed. His father was one exception. They'd warmly accepted him and called him the Crazy Fox. He didn't care. He adopted the name, painted his pictures of the island and its peoples, and entertained his son in the summer.

The other exception was Nicholas Scarlotti, who had nearly destroyed the island.

Jana watched Trevor closely as he flipped switches and turned dials in preparation for landing. Her mind was racing, planning ahead. She had a rough idea where the bank robbers were staying. Uncle Nicky's informants had supplied that information. It wasn't far from the airport. Then again, from what Uncle Nicky had told her, nothing was far from the airport.

She glanced out the window at the rapidly approaching landing strip. Calling this an airport seemed as ridiculous as calling the scattering of houses off to her right a town. The runway looked more like a wide section of highway that had been plopped down on the end of the island. It started abruptly and ended just as abruptly, and the closer they came, the shorter it looked.

The first bump as the plane's wheels touched down nearly jarred the gun from her hand. The plane lifted, then touched down again with another jarring bounce. She was prepared this time.

On the runway ahead, a paper bag blew across the tarmac. "Bit of a breeze out there, I'd say," she shouted, hoping nothing big decided to blow into them as Trevor slowed the plane.

"It's going to get worse," he answered curtly, never looking away from the runway. "Only an idiot flies *into* a hurricane."

She got the message. "We'll be out of here as soon as we get Jeff."

"Well, you'd better make it fast."

The plane slowed to taxiing speed, and he turned it back toward the one building she'd seen. It looked like a shack. "We're just going to get my stepbrother and leave," she assured him.

"You still haven't told me how you plan to do that."

"I'll let you know when the time comes."

He looked at her, his blond eyebrows rising slightly, and she had a feeling he'd guessed she didn't have a plan. "I know where they are," she said. "It's a house on the edge of town. Uncle Nicky's source said there were five men staying there. It has to be the four robbers and Jeff."

"'Has to be'? You mean, you're not sure?"

"I'm pretty sure."

"Oh, great." He turned off the engine and twisted in his seat to face her. "You pull a gun on me, hijack my plane, and fly us into a hurricane, and you're not even sure if your brother's here."

Jana stiffened at his accusation. "As I said, I'm pretty sure he's here. The five men were described as three whites and two blacks. That's a perfect match to the robbers and my stepbrother. And this isn't a hurricane. Not yet." She glanced out the window. The trees behind the shack they were now parked in front of were swaying wildly in the wind. Maybe it wasn't a hurricane, but it was rapidly building to one. They had to move fast.

"Get out." She motioned with her gun and released her seat belt. "Slowly and carefully."

He hesitated a moment, then shook his head as he released his seat belt. Squeezing past her, he headed for the back of the plane and the door. She quickly followed, leaving her leather handbag and camera. For now the gun was all she needed.

"Step away from the plane," she ordered when he

reached the tarmac. Then, keeping her eyes on him, she carefully descended herself, praying she didn't lose her balance and fall.

He walked toward the shack, and she panicked. "Stop where you are!"

"I've got to get chocks for the wheels." He smiled smugly. "You don't want this plane rolling off without us, do you?"

She didn't bother to answer that. "Get what you need," she said, and followed him.

From the shack, he grabbed two sets of wedges from the pile near the wall and carried them back to the plane. "You know," he said, slipping the chocks into place around the wheels, "considering how fast this hurricane is coming in, I really should stay here with the plane. If that wind picks up much more, these chocks aren't going to help. And you won't be taking your stepbrother anywhere if we lose the plane."

Jana chuckled. "Nice try, Fox," she said, admiring the way he'd sounded so sincere and concerned. "Do you really think I'd let you stay here by yourself? I'm not that stupid. Two minutes and you'd be out of here."

Trevor stood and brushed his hands on his pant legs, then smiled at her. "It was worth a try."

The wind blew a strand of his hair down over his forehead. He pushed it back, watching her. The wind was whipping her hair across her face too. She ignored it.

They were on land now, he mused, in no danger of crashing. Size-wise, he could easily overpower her. The gun in her hand was the equalizer. He wasn't 100 percent convinced she'd use it, but he wasn't sure she wouldn't.

He decided a game of wait and see would be safest. "So where to, lady?"

She glanced to his left and nodded. "That way. But we've got to keep from being seen."

Considering that they were the only two people on the landing strip and there were no other planes around, he had a feeling blending into the crowd might be a bit difficult. On the other hand, the wind seemed to be keeping the islanders inside. The village looked deserted.

Cayton—population 126, give or take a birth or death—wasn't much of a town. There was the church, built back at the turn of the century, Groaners Bar, Cora's trading post, the bait shop, and the ice plant. They were all located by the docks. Otherwise, most of the islanders did business out of their houses, trading and selling their handicrafts for products they needed.

Cayton's brightly painted wooden houses followed no residential plan. Scattered here and there, they were connected by twisting roads that more closely resembled dirt paths than streets. Some had sheds that housed the goats or cows the islanders raised. All had gardens and chickens to supply the vegetables and fresh eggs that rounded out their mostly fish diet.

Fishing was the primary occupation on the island, and the village had spread from the dock area to the woods and no farther. Beyond the pines and palms that fringed the village, the island turned hostile, the swamps harboring mosquitoes big enough to carry off a small child. At least that's what the islanders had told him the first summer he came to visit his father.

Curiosity, though, had taken him into those woods

and through the swamps, and at the age of sixteen, curiosity had led him to the limestone cave that faced the sea. There he'd learned a secret that almost cost him his life.

It was ironic that Nicholas Scarlotti was again, in a way, threatening his life. Ironic that he was more intrigued than frightened by the woman holding a gun on him. He glanced back at Jana. She was looking toward the town.

"Which house?" he asked as they neared the woods.

"The one nearest the shoreline and next to the woods."

He stopped and faced her, frowning. "That's where my father lived."

"I know."

He stayed motionless, staring at her. She knew far too much about him, and the look in her eyes said she didn't like what she'd heard. Once again, he'd been judged and condemned by his past.

He turned away and cut through the trees, the brush higher than it had been years ago but the journey familiar. He knew who lived in the first house that bordered the edge of town, knew who lived in each of the houses they skirted. The only unknown was his father's house.

Five years earlier his father had died, and Trevor had stopped coming to the island. He'd kept thinking he would return, but he never had. Sometimes he blamed it on a lack of time. Sometimes on a lack of money. Mostly, he thought, it was a reticence to face the past.

Now he was here.

"Stop," Jana ordered, her voice lower.

He stopped. Above the wind, they could hear a hammering sound. She pointed at the yellow house that looked out over the water. "The sound seems to be coming from there," she said, edging closer. "That's the house, isn't it? Your father's house?"

"That's it." He glanced down and saw her attention was on the house, not him. This was the opportunity he'd been waiting for, the moment to change who was in command.

He shifted his weight, ready to grab her arm and twist the gun out of her hand. Just as quickly, her attention snapped back to him, the barrel of the gun pointing directly at his midsection.

He smiled; she smiled back. "How close can we get without being seen?" she asked.

"Fairly close." He mentally kicked himself for not acting faster. Old age was catching up with him. Back in the days when he'd been in the marines, he wouldn't have let himself get in this position, much less have remained in it this long.

"The woods go right up next to the house?" she asked.

"Within ten feet." He remembered how scared he'd been the first summer he visited his father, how sure he'd been that the chickcharnies the islanders had told him about would sneak out of those woods and carry him off. Even when his father assured him that the elfin creatures didn't really exist, he'd worried about what might be living in the bogs. Not until he was older and had traveled every inch of the island had he lost that fear.

"I want to get close," Jana said, "close enough to see who's there and where they have Jeff."

"And then what? Do you think they'll just let him come out and play?"

She scowled at him, not answering.

"You still haven't told me your plan."

She waved the gun. "My plan is to get closer."

He led the way, taking them nearer to the house. Anyone looking their direction would have seen them, two bodies slipping from one tree to the next, but as far as he could tell, no one was looking. All the windows of the yellow house had blinds that were closed or partially closed. The occupants seemed less interested in looking out than keeping others from looking in. There was no way of telling how many men might be in the house or where they might be keeping their hostage . . . if they had a hostage.

He guided Jana as close to the front of the house as he could. The sound of hammering had grown louder with each step they took, and now they could see two men on the veranda nailing boards over the windows that looked out on the sea. Trevor recognized one of the men. He'd played with Steve Romi when they were both in their teens, and had heard that Steve had left the island to work at one of the hotels in Nassau. That had been years ago.

Trevor had a feeling Steve wasn't working for any hotel now, not unless he'd been hired by hotel security. Steve and the other man were wearing shoulder holsters carrying thirty-eights.

Any doubts he'd had about Jana's story disappeared, and Trevor was glad the two men hadn't noticed they were being observed. He edged back a little, forcing Jana to stay behind him and out of sight.

The two men were obviously preparing for the winds that were growing stronger. Out along the shoreline, a hundred feet from the house, the incoming tide was eating up the sand, each wave rising higher than the last. The islanders had always told Trevor's father he shouldn't have glass in his windows, that you needed to give the spirits a way in and out of the house. His father had just smiled and ignored the warnings. He'd also had to board up his windows every time a storm approached.

"Should just break these windows out," Steve yelled to the other man, his voice carrying on the wind. "Last hurricane, all those windows in the hotels in Nassau, they breaks. Hotels have to close down, let their workers go. I don't like windows. We never have them in my father's house. Winds go through. Everybody fine. You know what I mean, man?"

"He wants them boarded up," the other man yelled back, his skin as dark as Steve's. "He wants to stay a little while longer. I'm gettin' sick of doin' what *he* wants."

He hit his thumb with his hammer and began cussing. The front door opened, and a tall, lean man wearing glasses stepped out, his light skin a dramatic contrast to the other two men. For a moment, the man looked toward the woods, and Trevor sucked in a breath, afraid they might have been seen.

Next to him, he heard Jana also take in a breath.

Trevor glanced her way and noticed the pistol was now pointed toward the ground, not at him. It was the opportunity he'd been waiting for, the moment he could overpower her with little or no danger to his safety.

He didn't move.

Jana was staring at the veranda, her eyes wide and her lips parted. Her expression told Trevor who the man with the glasses was. In her eyes, he saw her surprise, her disbelief, her pain, and he could understand every tortured emotion flowing through her. Betrayal ate deep into a person's being. She'd come to rescue her stepbrother. Now she knew the truth.

"That's him . . ." she said, looking at Trevor. "That's Jeff."

THREE

Jana didn't know what to do. Standing on the porch, talking casually with his supposed abductors, was her stepbrother. Not only that, he seemed to be in charge.

For the last two months, she'd worried about him. Day after day, she'd feared for his life and had blamed herself for his kidnapping. Even when the police and FBI had suggested he might have been involved, she'd staunchly defended Jeff. The call and ransom note Jeff's father had received seemed evidence enough that Jeff was an innocent bystander. No son would put his father through that kind of emotional hell, she'd argued.

Evidently Jeff would, Jana realized. What a fool she'd been. What a stupid fool.

The sight of another man running around the side of the house stopped her mental chastising. His blond hair shaved close to his head and his face pockmarked and scarred, he looked mean and ugly. Almost in unison the three on the veranda turned his way.

"There's a plane's on the airstrip," he yelled, and Jana recognized his voice, just as she'd recognized the voice of the man who'd hit his thumb with the hammer. During the robbery, Pock Face had been behind her, keeping her pinned to the floor while the thumb hitter had held a gun on Jeff and shoved him out of the bank.

"The police?" Jeff asked, stepping to the edge of the veranda and looking toward the village. "Coast Guard?"

"I don't think so," Pock Face said. "From what I heard it's a man and a woman."

"Maybe they're tourists," Thumb Hitter suggested.

Jeff glared at him. "And how many tourists have you seen fly in here in the last month?"

Jana felt Trevor's hand on her shoulder and realized she'd completely forgotten him, had forgotten to keep up her guard. She jerked to the side and aimed the gun at him. He held up his hands, but nodded toward the airstrip and mouthed a command. "We've got to get back to the plane."

She understood. But simply getting back to the plane wouldn't be enough. She couldn't leave without Jeff. More than ever she needed him to clear her name.

From the corner of her eye, she saw Jeff and the other two leave the veranda. Trevor also moved. Ignoring the gun she had pointed at him, he took off at a run back into the woods.

For a moment, she hesitated, then followed Trevor.

In high school she'd run track, but she'd given up the sport after graduating. Within minutes, she wished she'd continued those daily runs. Halfway back to the point where they'd entered the woods, she had to call out to Trevor. "I can't—" she gasped, fighting for her breath.

He looked back, then slowed and stopped, coming back to her. "We've got to get there before they do," he said.

"I know. I just—" She leaned over, gulping in air.

"I'll go on ahead."

He started to jog away, and Jana knew his was a reasonable idea. She was holding him back. But then, so many things had seemed reasonable only a while ago. She no longer knew what to believe or whom to trust.

Quickly she straightened, again aiming the gun at him. "No. We go together."

He frowned when he glanced back and saw the gun. "If they get the plane—"

He didn't have to finish. She understood. "We go together," she repeated, and forced herself to start up again, even though her lungs were screaming for relief and a pain in her side wouldn't go away.

They were barely more than a football field away from the airstrip when Trevor slowed to a stop. The trees they were using for cover had thinned to a few. Ahead was the open stretch of sand and grass, then the tarmac, then the plane. "I think we got here first," he said, glancing toward the village. "Can you make a dash to the plane?"

"I think so." Actually, she saw no other choice. "Yes."

"On the count of—"

He stopped, and Jana understood why. A man had stepped around from the backside of the plane. Even at a distance, she could see he was carrying a rifle—a rifle and her leather handbag. The fourth robber, she realized. The other white man. And once again, he was robbing her. He was holding all of her life savings in that leather bag.

"What are we going to do?" she gasped, the wind whipping her hair across her eyes.

"Hey, you're the one calling the shots," Trevor snapped, glancing down at the gun she still held pointed at his midsection.

She was in command. But of what? Certainly not the situation. Nothing was working out right. She was tempted to hand him the gun. Why not? Maybe he could fire it if necessary. She didn't think she could. Maybe he could come up with an idea to get them out of this mess.

"I'll tell you what," she started.

She didn't have a chance to finish.

"No, I'll tells you what," a man said from behind them. "You puts down that gun and slowly turns around."

Jana glanced at Trevor. His nod said to comply, and she slowly placed on the ground the 9 mm semiautomatic she'd been so sure would guarantee her safety. Then she turned around.

It was Thumb Hitter, but instead of a hammer, he was now holding a thirty-eight. "Whadja two thinks you was gonna do?" he asked, smiling triumphantly. "Sneak back and fly off without saying hello?"

Trevor stepped away from her, his hands in the air. "Hey, man. Leave me out of this," he said, clearly putting a distance between them. "I had nothing to do with this. You can see that, can't you? She had that gun on me. Hijacked my plane. Made me fly her here."

The gunman glanced at her pistol on the ground, then at Trevor. "You telling me, man, that you let a woman hijack your plane?"

"What can I say? I was duped by a pretty face."

Jana glared at Trevor. Uncle Nicky had been right. The guy was scum. Trevor was even moving closer to the gunman, aligning himself with the enemy.

Thumb Hitter smiled and glanced to his left. "Got yore little sister," he yelled toward the nearest houses.

She saw them then, Jeff and the other two, coming across the open stretch between the village and the woods. She'd not only failed to rescue her stepbrother, she was now going to be his hostage. "I'm not his little sister," she snapped.

Trevor inched closer to the gunman. The man wasn't watching him as closely as he should be. The whining had worked, along with his confession of being duped by a pretty face. Thumb Hitter saw him as a victim, not a threat.

That was the way Trevor wanted it.

He knew they would have little chance of escape once the others were there. Now all he had to hope was his training in the marines would pay off. It had been a long time since he'd played soldier.

He moved quickly, using the element of surprise. A karate kick with his right foot hit the gunman's hand, sending the thirty-eight flying. Then a quick downward chop to the neck with his right hand put the man on the ground. Immediately, he reached out and grabbed Jana's hand, pulling her up from where she'd crouched. Half dragging her, he led her back into the woods.

He ran in a zigzagging pattern, praying if anyone shot at them, the trees would block a bullet. He felt Jana stumble and lurch, but amazingly she kept up. Only when they'd run deep into a stand of madeira trees did she gasp a protest.

"No more!" she cried, and he stopped, his own lungs aching and his legs leadened.

Fighting to bring his breathing back to normal, he listened. The wind whistling through the tops of the trees made hearing difficult, but somewhere in the distance someone yelled. They were being followed, and their pursuers weren't that far away.

Trevor looked at Jana. Her cheeks were flushed, and each breath she took pressed her breasts against the silk of her blouse, perspiration dampening the blue fabric and making it cling to her skin. There wasn't as much cleavage exposed as he'd seen earlier that day. Sometime or another, between getting on his plane and now, she'd buttoned some of the buttons. Not that covering up her chest subtracted from her allure. With her hair tangled and her lips parted, she looked like a woman in the throes of lovemaking.

To his surprise, he felt a tightening in his loins.

Off to their left came another shout. The answering call was closer yet. Trevor took Jana's hand again and started off. Tired or not, they had no choice. They had to keep going.

A rumble, deep and resonant, traveled through the sky, and he felt the first drops of rain. He ignored them. He was heading for the marsh, every step a familiar reminder of his past. An absence of five years hadn't erased his memory of the island. He knew its contours as a man knew a lover. While Sean Fox had covered canvas after canvas with colorful images, Trevor had investigated the island's limestone cliffs and boggy marshes. Summer after summer, the harsh terrain and swampy wetlands that kept tourists away had been his playground.

He led Jana directly into the marsh, guiding her over one tangle of roots to another. The rain increased, a drizzle becoming a downpour, and he knew it was a blessing. Tracks that might have given them away were washed clean. Mosquitoes that would have eaten them alive had been driven to shelter.

Slowly, they progressed, each step taking them deeper into the bog. "Watch out for snakes," he called back to her.

"Snakes!" She stopped, her hand slipping free from his.

Trevor looked back at her, a frown creasing his brow. "What? Are you going to play Miss Scaredy-cat now?"

She lifted her chin. "No."

"Just stay close."

Easier said than done, Jana realized as he moved effortlessly from one high spot to the next. Her progress was less positive, each step accompanied by a glance to make sure there were no snakes in the trees or in the water. The path he was guiding her along was more a tangle of roots than sand or ground. On either side of her was a muddy, sandy bog, filled with sargasso weeds, and it reeked with the stench of stagnant water. One misstep and she would be in that muck.

That Trevor could navigate the marsh with such ease impressed her. And his quick thinking earlier had saved them from becoming Jeff's prisoners. One moment she'd thought Trevor a scumbag, the next he was acting like a hero. She sure didn't understand men. Why couldn't they be what they appeared to be?

A flapping sound startled her. She gasped and misstepped, her foot sliding off the roots and sinking into mud. Two egrets, elegant and regal, spread their wings and flew off, but Jana barely noticed. Her foot was stuck, her first attempt to pull it free futile.

She tried again, with no success. Her sneaker was mired in the muddy sand, and Trevor was moving on, unaware of her plight.

She tugged and she pulled, then she saw the slithering form gliding through the water toward her.

Her scream pierced the rain and the wind. Desperately she tried to free her foot. The snake was coming closer, its dark outline barely making a ripple.

"What the—" Trevor raced back toward her.

"Snake!" she cried, pointing at the water.

"Where?"

"There."

"That?" Trevor leaned over and scooped a long, slimy twig from the water.

Seeing her venomous viper was no more than a tree branch, Jana felt her heartbeat slow a fraction, but it didn't ease the tension running through her. She was out

of her element here. Over her head. She wanted out.
Wanted the nightmare to end.

Trevor dropped the twig back into the water, then
glared at her. "You keep yelling and your stepbrother is
going to know exactly where we are."

"Then get me out of here!" she demanded, tired of
fighting a losing battle. She gave another tug, but her
foot stayed mired in the mud.

He shook his head, and she could almost hear him
asking if there was anything else she could do wrong. She
didn't think so.

With one simple maneuver, Trevor broke the suction
and pulled her foot free, then without another word, he
started off again.

As she followed him, she realized she'd done one
thing right. She hadn't pulled out her gun and shot at the
twig. That certainly would have alerted Jeff to their
whereabouts.

Tapping the side pocket of her slacks, she felt the
reassuring outline of her pistol. In the instant Trevor had
kicked the gun from the robber's hand, she'd knelt and
retrieved her own. She wasn't totally helpless.

The feeling was reassuring.

Trevor didn't stop until they were out of the marsh
and on solid ground. Jana willingly stopped too. In silence they listened.

She heard nothing. No voices. No footsteps. Only the
wind and the rain and the rumble of thunder.

Raindrops streamed down her face and soaked her clothing. Trevor moved on, and again she followed.

"There's a place I know where we can find shelter," he said, surprising her with the sound of his voice. "It's not far."

"Okay."

She studied his back as she followed him. He wasn't unduly tall, probably close to six feet, but the width of his shoulders and his muscular build made him look big. She watched the play of his muscles beneath his rain-soaked shirt. She'd known that Trevor could easily overpower her if she let down her guard. Seeing him down that gunman had emphasized that reality. In that instant, she'd known both fear and love. She would have kissed him if there had been time.

Not that he would have welcomed a kiss.

She could imagine what he thought of her. Not only had she hijacked his plane, she'd forced him to fly into a hurricane, and now men with guns were chasing after him. Oh yes, he'd certainly welcome a kiss. He was probably considering ways to strangle her, and she wasn't sure she'd blame him.

Everything had gone wrong.

She noticed they were climbing, the trees around them giving way to rocky outcroppings of limestone and thick brush. When Trevor stopped, she nearly ran into him, her hand touching his back before she realized what she was doing. His body was warm, and just as quickly as she'd touched him, she jerked her hand back.

He turned and looked down at her, his expression cold. "There's an entrance to a cave somewhere around here," he said. "It would give us a place to get out of this rain, and I know no one would find us. I'm not even sure I can find it. This brush has really grown since the last time I was here."

"How big a cave is this?" On either side of them were massive boulders and dense brush, but she didn't see anything that resembled a cave.

"Not very big. Actually, it's a space between two rocks. The opening is only about this high off the ground." He indicated midthigh with his hand. "Inside there's more room. The Arawaks used it."

"Arawaks?"

He nodded. "The Arawaks were the original inhabitants of the Bahamas. They lived here back before Columbus landed on these islands. Of course, within thirty years, Columbus and his successors had either killed them off or enslaved them."

"I don't see any signs of a cave or an opening."

"It's around here," he said, and began pulling brush back from the rocks, moving fallen branches, and sliding chunks of broken and crumbling limestone to the side.

For a moment she watched, then moved ahead of him and did the same. She pushed brush apart only to reveal a wall of rock. Moving a broken limb and a loose slab of limestone garnered nothing. She turned to the next section, pulled a bush back, and saw it.

Big and ugly, it crawled toward her, its orange throat puffed out. She screeched and jumped back, letting go of the bush. Loose, wet, talc-smooth sand shifted beneath her feet, and she felt herself falling. Arms flying, she landed on her rear end, the impact traveling up her spine and jarring her head.

"What the—" she heard Trevor mutter, then he swore.

"It's a—" she began.

"An iguana," he finished, disgust dripping from his words as he pulled back the branch so she could see the scaly, oversized lizard. "Harmless. Are you going to spook at everything around here? Or are you purposely trying to tell your stepbrother where we are?"

"I didn't know . . ." she started, then stopped. Giving excuses wouldn't help. Trevor was right. Yelling like that, she could have given them away. Her stepbrother and the others were far more dangerous than an iguana.

Trevor didn't offer to help her up, and noting his sullen expression, Jana didn't ask. She rose with as much dignity as she could muster and brushed off the seat of her cotton slacks. She could feel the grit and could imagine how she looked. Her rain-soaked hair was plastered to the sides of her face, her sneakers were covered with mud, and now her pants were dirty. It was a good thing she wasn't trying to lure him with her sex appeal now.

"I found it," he said flatly, and pushed a vine to the side, revealing a narrow opening between two rocks.

The hole wasn't much wider than Trevor's shoulders and barely as high as her waist. He motioned with his hand, and she understood. He expected her to go through the hole, to enter some dark unknown.

The idea of running into something else unknown sent a chill down her spine. She bowed politely. "After you."

"Scared of the dark as well as of everything else?" The lift of his eyebrows taunted her.

"Caution is not the same as fear."

"Might be a monster in there."

"Might be," she agreed. She was learning there were monsters everywhere, even in her family.

He grunted, then ducked down to crawl through the hole. She watched his back side disappear, then his legs and feet. The limestone swallowed him up, and she was left standing alone, the rain pouring down on her.

A crack of lightning prodded her to move. Taking in a deep breath, she crouched down and crawled through the opening.

As dark as the cloud-covered sky had been, it was darker in front of her. Inch by inch, she crept into a cool, inky nothingness. "Trevor?" she called, afraid he'd somehow vanished.

"Keep coming," he said. "You're blocking what little light there is."

She crawled forward, the crumbled limestone flooring rubbing across her palms and grating at her knees. A musty odor surrounded her, conjuring up images of dark cellars, bats, and spider webs. Once inside, she did notice a slight increase in visibility. She could make out Trevor's silhouette. He was standing.

Cautiously, she rose to her feet, checking with her hands to find the sides and height of the cave. Her fingertips touched rough stones, and from her estimate, Trevor barely cleared the ceiling.

"I don't imagine you have a flashlight," he said.

"In my bag." Which one of the robbers now had, she remembered.

"No cigarette lighter? Matches?"

"I don't smoke."

"Just hijack planes, is that it?"

"I'm sorry. I didn't mean to get you into this mess."

"You sure acted as though you mean it. I hope you realize hijacking is a federal offense."

"I was going to pay you."

"Wooptedoo." He didn't sound amused.

"I will pay you." She just had to get her leather bag back.

"And do you have any idea how we're going to get off this island?"

"I have a gun." She slipped the pistol out of her pocket, the feel of it in her hand reassuring.

"You dropped it, remember? Back when that guy told you to."

"Then picked it up when you were fighting with him."

"Oh yeah? If that's so, let me have it."

He sounded closer, and although the situation had changed from when she'd first pulled the gun on Trevor, the idea of actually handing the gun over to him gave her pause. "I—I think I'd better keep it."

"Why? So you can shoot me if I don't do what you want?"

He was definitely closer. She could sense his nearness, and stepped back. "I just think it's better if I keep it."

"And would you have shot me earlier?"

"I—" She wasn't sure how to answer.

"Would you shoot me now?"

She felt his hand touch the gun and heard his mutter of surprise. He hadn't really believed she had the gun, she realized. After that, things happened too quickly for her to piece together. One moment his hand was touching her arm, the next her wrist was being painfully twisted to the side. Her fingers spasmed, and she felt the trigger give. The jerk of the gun accompanied the bang. With a grunt, Trevor let go of her arm.

"Damn you," he swore, and in his words, she heard the pain and surprise.

"Oh, God." She felt the tears forming in her eyes. The day her father was shot, she'd cried until she couldn't cry anymore. She'd watched him die, the life seeping out of him. She couldn't even see Trevor.

She dropped the gun, her body shaking. "Trevor . . ."

FOUR

Trevor put his hand to his side. The cotton fibers of his shirt were frayed and the skin beneath tender. The realization of how close the bullet had come froze his blood. Half an inch closer and he would have had a hole in his side. More and he might now be fighting for his life.

"Are you—are you. . . ?" Jana stammered, her voice shaky.

"What? Alive?" He was beyond shaky, the adrenaline racing through his body mingling with anger. "Yes, I'm alive. No thanks to you."

He grabbed her arms, wanting to shake her, to somehow make her realize what she'd almost done. He felt her tremors and heard her gasps for breath. Digging his fingers into her soft flesh, he closed his eyes and fought for control.

"I didn't mean . . ." she said, her words half sobs. "I told them I wouldn't be able to . . . I'm not like them . . . All I wanted was to be a normal person, to have a decent job—"

Her voice didn't sound normal. "Jana?"

She kept on going. "I'd just gotten a promotion. No one knew about me at the bank. No one suspected."

Her entire body was shaking, her breathing shallow and coming in frantic gasps. Trevor knew what was happening. He'd seen hysteria before. It took over, wiping out all reason. Talking to her would do no good. She was beyond rational conversation, beyond comprehension. There was only one way to get through to her.

Over in Kuwait, he'd slapped a soldier who'd been overcome with fear. It had worked. Stunned, the man had listened to him and had understood what he was saying. After that, reason had calmed him.

Trevor released his hold on Jana's left arm and pulled back his right hand, then stopped himself. He'd never hit a woman before, and he wasn't about to begin now. Maybe she'd hurt him, but he didn't want to hurt her.

He chose another tactic.

In the darkness, he could barely make out her silhouette, but he easily caught a handful of her wet hair, drew her close, and tilted her head back. Pressed against his body, her breasts flattened, and he could feel as well as hear her catch her breath. He found and captured her mouth with his own. Startled, she started to protest, the sound swallowed before it escaped.

Though she struggled to get away, he held on, kissing her with a fervor that surprised him. What had started as therapy was rapidly changing. One touch of her lips, and he was the one losing reasoning powers. Anger was replaced by desire, his body physically responding to her. He softened the kiss and loosened his hold on her hair. If she wanted to escape, he would let her. Another thing he'd never done was force a woman.

She didn't pull back. Instead, she touched his arms. Cautiously, at first, then firmly holding onto him. And as she did, her lips moved with his.

He tasted the salt of her tears and wanted to know more. As if understanding, she opened to him, allowing him entry. He accepted the invitation, thrusting his tongue deep into the moist warmth of her mouth, and at the same time, he completely released his hold on her hair, sliding his hands down to her bottom. There, too, he pressed, bringing her hips against his. His desire was a hard bulge that neither of them could ignore.

The fiery heat racing through his body matched a need he hadn't felt in months . . . maybe years. From the moment he'd looked up from his coffee that morning and watched her walk toward his office, she'd aroused him. Nothing she'd done had changed that. Physically, he wanted her, wanted to strip her clothes from her body and make love to her.

He stepped forward, forcing her to take a step back. His hand touched the smooth, cool limestone first, and he edged even closer, using the unyielding wall to keep her pressed against his body while his hands were free to remove her clothing. He fumbled with the buttons of her rain-soaked blouse as he kissed the side of her neck. Her skin was wet and warm, its floral scent filling his nostrils. He felt her hands pressing against his arms, pushing, but he ignored the pressure, his needs driving him on.

"Trevor!"

The panic in her voice had a different tone from before. He ignored it, concentrating instead on stripping the wet silk blouse away from her chest. He found the lacy edging of her bra and slid his hands over the soft, firm mounds of her breasts. Her nipples pressed hard through wet nylon, and he rubbed his palms over them, delighting in the feel and smiling when she groaned in pleasure.

He wanted to taste her, to suck on those nipples; wanted to fill her with his need, plunging himself deep within her. He started to slip her bra straps from her shoulders. She wiggled against him and whispered a plea. "Trevor, please . . . no."

He didn't want to listen, didn't want to comply. She didn't mean it, he told himself. He deserved this.

"Please, no," she repeated, her fear palpable.

The realization of what he was doing shocked him, and he pushed himself away from Jana and turned his back to her. He heard her ragged breathing and knew his was as uneven. Staring into the darkness, he forced his body to relax and prayed she wouldn't talk. His nerves were on edge, his reactions too unstable. Control was a thin thread, and his had nearly snapped.

"Trevor?"

Her voice was hesitant. He growled his response. "Don't talk. Don't say anything."

"But—"

"Nothing," he repeated, and struggled to rein in his hormones.

When she said nothing, he nodded to himself. At

least he'd gain control over her. That was a nice change. Somewhere on the floor of this cave was a gun. This time he wanted it in *his* possession. Kneeling, he felt around. The moment he touched the cold metal, his fingers tightened around the grip. He felt until he found the safety. She evidently hadn't had it on. He made sure it was in place.

Once he had the gun, he walked over to the entrance to the cave and crouched to look out. The rain had lessened, the thunderstorm moving on, but it was still windy. The branches of the brush in front of the opening kept blowing across his line of vision. He was pleased. As difficult as it had been for him to find what he knew was here, he was sure that if Jana's stepbrother or the others happened along this way, they wouldn't see the opening. They were safe, at least from the others, if not from each other.

His own tension easing, he sank down on the floor of the cave, using the wall near the entrance to rest his back. Roughly ten feet separated him from Jana. He needed that distance. "We've got a problem," he said. She didn't respond, and he went on. "We've got to get back to my plane and get off this island before they take it."

"I can't leave without Jeff," she said, her voice still unsteady.

"Forget Jeff."

"I can't." Her tone was stronger. "Without Jeff, I might as well stay here in this cave. I can't go back to the states. If I'm not thrown in jail, Senor Alvarez or one of his men will get me."

"So what are you going to do, go back and say, 'Hey,

Jeff, I'm in big trouble because of you, so would you mind turning yourself in so the heat's off me?'"

"You're mocking me."

"No, I'm trying to make you face facts, honey. Your stepbrother is not willingly going to go with you."

"So I have to figure a way to make him unwillingly go with me."

"One against five?" Her assumption that she could succeed was ridiculous.

"I have no choice. Besides, I do have a gun." She sank to her knees and began feeling around in front of her.

"No, I have your gun."

Jana stopped running her hands over the crumbled limestone. She had seen him drop to his knees before he went over to the opening. She should have realized what he was doing. He would have heard her drop the gun after it went off. Of course he'd looked for it. Now he had it, and she had nothing. Sitting back, she found a position against the rocks, sighed, and rebuttoned her blouse. "Well, maybe you can use it to get your plane back."

"Damn right I will. I'm certainly not giving it back to you. Next time you might kill me."

"I didn't mean for that to happen. If you hadn't grabbed my arm—"

"I was getting a little tired of your waving that thing in my face."

"I wasn't waving it." She stopped. This was getting them nowhere. "How bad are you hit?"

"The bullet grazed me," he said. "Gave me a burn mark. That's bad enough, in my opinion."

"I'm sorry," she said again. Hurting him had never been her intention.

"Sorry doesn't cut it."

She heard him expel a breath and knew he was still angry. "I thought the safety was on," she added.

He scoffed.

"I'm not used to guns. I'm not used to any of this."

"Sure, and that's why you call a known mobster *Uncle* Nicky."

Explaining her relationship to Nicholas Scarlotti was not going to be easy. "I wouldn't have turned to him if I'd had a choice. My mother and I vowed we would never have anything to do with the Family, never again. We even changed our names."

"So your name's not Jenkins, either?"

"Legally it is, but when I was born, I was christened Jana Maria Capolli. My father was Angelo Capolli." She paused, waiting to see if he recognized the name, but not really expecting him to. The FBI, of course, had known the name well. As they'd told her two months earlier, they had a file on him. Had a file on her mother and on her. They might have thought they'd disappeared, but their every move had been followed.

Later she'd discovered that even the Family knew all about them. They'd been watched from the day they left Chicago. Been watched, reported on, and protected. How foolish she and her mother had been. You didn't escape the Family. Ever.

"My father worked for the Mob," she went on. "He was one of their enforcers."

"Enforcers?"

"He enforced the tariffs, the edicts. Whatever needed enforcing. Mom knew what he did. I didn't. I'll say this much for my father, he didn't involve us in the Family. But then, that's part of their code. Don't tell the wives or the children what you're doing. That way, if something goes wrong with the marriage, there's no danger of the Family business being broadcast to the wrong people. I knew a few of the people who came over to see my father, but not many. Uncle Nicky was one of them."

"So what happened to your father?" Trevor asked.

"He was killed. Shot. Right in front of our house. I didn't see it, but I heard the shot. At first I thought it was a car backfiring, then I heard my mother scream. I found her out on the lawn, kneeling on the grass and holding my father's head in her lap. I stood there, watching my mother cry and my father die, the blood oozing out of his body. It was terrible."

"How old were you?"

"Eleven."

Trevor blew out a breath. This was definitely not your everyday lady from a nice, average middle-class family. "And after your father died?"

"Mom decided we had to get out of Chicago. Two days after my father was buried, she told me to pack everything I absolutely had to have, that we were leaving and not coming back. Four hours later, in the dead of night, we were in a car headed south. She took us to Kentucky first. There she found a job, and we went before a judge and had our last names officially changed to Jenkins. She got all new identification for both of us. The next summer, we moved to Orlando. There she met a man from Michigan. He was nice. Older than my dad had been. A lot older. When spring came and he got ready to go back up to Michigan, he asked my mother and me to go with him. We did. I think Mom thought she was safe by then. We hadn't heard from the Family at all."

"But they were still around?"

"Not that we knew it, but it seems they were. When all this happened with the bank robbery and I finally went to Uncle Nicky, he knew everything we had been doing." She sighed. "He even knew Jeff was involved. He tried to tell me—I realize that now—but I wouldn't listen. I thought I knew Jeff so well. I'd been there during the robbery, I'd seen Jeff's face. He was as scared as I was."

She stopped, but Trevor didn't say anything. He knew she needed time to work this out in her mind. He'd been duped enough times to understand how difficult it was to accept when someone you trusted stabbed you in the back. You gave them your trust—fell in love with them—then learned the truth. Finding out you'd been a fool was a hard lesson to swallow.

"I guess Jeff's a pretty good actor," she finally said. "A heck of a lot better than I ever realized."

"How'd he happen to be in the bank working on your computer, anyway?"

"Now that I look back, I can see he set it up way ahead of that day. One night when I was having dinner with Mom and my stepfather, Jeff was there. I told him about a new program I had and the problems I'd been having with it. Jeff said he could help me, that in exchange for a dinner out, he'd give me a training session and make sure the program didn't have any bugs. He'd asked me out before, but I'd always turned him down. He just isn't my type. But this time, since he is an expert with computers, it sounded like a good idea to me. And he is my stepbrother."

"Jeff is the son of the man your mother went to Michigan with?"

"No. It's more complicated than that. Gordon, the man Mom met in Florida, died a couple years after we moved to Michigan. As I said, he was quite a bit older than she, childless, and financially well-off. Even though he never married Mom, he put her in his will, and she got a nice sum of money. Enough to buy a house, send me to college, and pay the bills. I was already working when Mom met and married Fred, Jeff's dad. Fred's a nice guy." She stopped. "At least, I always thought he was a nice guy. Now I don't know about anyone."

"I'm a nice guy."

"You just tried to rape me."

"I did not," he said, though he knew it had come close to that.

"You could have fooled me."

"You said you were easily fooled."

"Some things I know." She sighed. "Why did you kiss me, anyway?"

"You were hysterical. It was that or slap you."

She said nothing, and he wished he had slapped her. Too much had been revealed in that kiss. "What did you expect, anyway? The way you looked and acted in my office this morning, you were asking for that."

"I wasn't asking for anything but a plane ride."

"Sure, honey."

"Uncle Nicky said you'd be easily duped by a pretty face and a lot of money."

"So you played the sex kitten and flashed a wad of hundreds in my face."

"It worked, didn't it?"

He hated to admit it had. With a grunt, he changed the subject. "I want to know more about your step-brother. If you didn't tell him your password, how did he get into the bank's system and transfer money?"

"I wish I knew."

"Did you have it written down on your desk?"

"No. It wasn't that hard to remember. We needed at least seven letters and one number, and I was exhausted when I got to work and found out I had to come up with a new password, so I typed in IAM2TIRED, using the number two for too."

"You must have mentioned it to Jeff."

"I didn't." She sighed again. "You sound like the FBI agent who kept interrogating me. As I told him, Jeff wouldn't have had a clue what my password was. That's why I was so sure he was innocent. Boy, what a sucker I was."

"One is born every minute, they say."

"Seems so."

"Add me to the group. 'I want to check out possible film locations,'" he said, mocking her voice and fake excuse for hiring his plane. "How could I be so lucky?"

"Oh, don't play the innocent." She snorted her disgust. "I know all about you."

"And what do you know?"

"That you were caught transporting drugs when you were in the marines and that's why you were kicked out."

"I didn't know there were illegal drugs on that plane," he insisted. "I thought we were taking medical supplies to that village. And I wasn't kicked out. I was given a dishonorable discharge."

"Big difference." She didn't sound convinced. "And what about your being arrested in that hotel with that woman who was known to be a drug dealer?"

"A combination of another pretty face and bad timing."

"Uncle Nicky told me not to worry about hijacking your plane, that you're nothing more than a drug runner."

"Me? I have never knowingly run drugs, no matter what anyone thinks. But let me tell you, if anyone should know about running drugs, it's your Uncle Nicky. What do you think he was doing when he lived on this island, taking a vacation?" Trevor scoffed at the idea. "He nearly killed me the time I found his stash."

"If Uncle Nicky had wanted you dead, you would be."

"Trust me, he did a good job of scaring the pants off a sixteen-year-old. Maybe he's still planning on getting rid of me. Why else send you to me?"

"Maybe because—because . . ." She paused, and when she spoke again, her tone was pensive. "Maybe because he thought you'd help me."

"Yeah? Well if so, why didn't he just have you come right out and tell me what was up and ask for my help?"

"If I had, would you have helped me?"

"Hell no."

She laughed, the sound softer and more relaxed than before. "No, I didn't think you would, and I don't think Uncle Nicky thought you would, either. He said I'd have to use money, that you needed money. Money and a little sex appeal."

"And I fell for it."

"And you've helped me." She paused. "Thank you for getting us away from that gunman."

"It was my hide I was protecting."

"You didn't have to take me with you. You could have run off on your own, left me there."

"Yeah, well, I don't do those kinds of things."

"I think Uncle Nicky knew that."

"Look, honey, don't make me a saint, or him one, either."

"I'm not." She sounded more assured. "But it's good to know I have an ally. Now, as far as I can figure, what we've got to do is go back to your father's house. Once we're there, we'll have to create some sort of diversion, something that will get all of them out of the house. Once Jeff is outside, we can grab him and get him back to the plane. After that, we're home free."

"Honey, you make it sound so easy."

"It would help if we could get the money back that I had in my bag. I mean, that was for you, and I don't have any more. I had to clean out my savings account to get that much."

"So all we do is leave this cave, go to my father's house, lure your stepbrother out, grab him, and fly him back to Florida." He hoped she heard how absurd it all sounded.

"That's basically it."

She was either totally dense or ridiculously optimistic. "It's not going to happen."

"Why not?"

"First of all because I want no part of it." All he wanted was to get his plane back. That was going to be hard enough to manage.

"But we've got to—"

"No, honey, there's no *we* in this. Whether your uncle Nicky sent you to me for help or because he wants to torture me, I don't know, but I'm not a part of this. The only 'got to' I'm interested in is I've got to get my plane back."

"But without Jeff—"

"You tell the authorities what you discovered here and let them take over."

"But Senor Alvarez . . . "

"Will have to deal with your stepbrother."

"I don't think you understand about Senor Alvarez."

"I don't think you understand how dangerous your stepbrother and those four men are."

He heard her sigh and hoped the silence that followed was an indication that she was seriously thinking about all he'd said.

"I guess you're right," she said. "When should we start back?"

Something about her compliance bothered him. It had come too quickly and easily. He hoped she was convinced, that she understood her plan was crazy. Suicidal. Even with her gun, they were outnumbered. No, what they had to concentrate on was getting his plane back. That was going to be difficult enough. "If you're rested," he said, "we should start back now."

FIVE

"Oh, geez." Jana stared at the tear in the side of Trevor's shirt. The fibers were frayed and scorched and sticking to his side. She reached out, cautiously touching the wound she'd caused.

He jerked away. "Leave it alone."

"You're bleeding."

He lifted his arm and glanced down at his side. "Barely."

"It should be cleaned."

"Later." He stepped away from her and started back along the trail they'd come up earlier.

"I really am sorry," she said, following him.

He didn't look back, and she wasn't sure if what he grumbled was "Forget it" or something more graphic.

She couldn't blame him for swearing at her, and she couldn't forget that she'd shot him. No more than she could forget the warmth of his lips or how his body had felt pressed against hers.

At first, his kiss had been forceful and angry. He'd shocked her out of her hysteria, all right. Even as upset as she'd been, she'd realized if he could kiss like that, he wasn't dying. But almost immediately his kiss had changed, had gentled and become more sensual.

That was the moment she should have said no and pushed him away. Instead she'd stood where she was, had reached for him and kissed him back. Her response didn't make any sense.

She didn't want to get involved with a man who lived on the edge of respectability. She'd been there once. Perhaps she'd been a child then, but she'd seen what loving someone like her father had done to her mother. Jana didn't want to give her heart to a man, only to have him die in her arms.

As she followed Trevor into the marsh, she mentally replayed those few minutes when he'd kissed her and how she'd reacted. Her responses to Trevor's kiss, she decided, were based on fear. Fear and relief. The fear that she'd killed him and the relief that she hadn't. Mix the two emotions with a dose of adrenaline and a dark cave, and you got crazy reactions. Kissing. Touching.

Wanting.

It all made sense when analyzed in the light of day. What didn't make sense was why simply remembering that kiss and the feel of Trevor's hands on her breasts had her skin on fire and her pulse racing. She knew she had to get her emotions under control, but watching Trevor as he strode ahead of her wasn't helping. Her gaze dropped to his chinos, still wet from the rain. The tan cotton clung to his body, and she closed her eyes, remembering the feel of him. The hard bulge beneath his slacks had definitely made his desires clear.

Her toe hit something solid, and she grunted as she stumbled, quickly opening her eyes. Trevor glanced back. "What?"

She felt her cheeks flame red. "Nothing. I tripped on a root."

"Well, stay alert. Your stepbrother and the others may still be looking for us."

He turned away and kept going, and Jana knew that if he'd wanted her in the cave, the urge had passed. She could spend her time fantasizing about what might have happened if she hadn't stopped him, could fall on her face walking around with her eyes closed, but he had put that moment behind him. Getting back to his plane was all he cared about now.

He had his plan.

She had to come up with one of her own.

She had to find a way to convince Trevor to forget about his plane, at least for the moment. She was not going back to the States without Jeff—she couldn't—and she needed both Trevor and that plane to get her stepbrother back.

The more she thought about it, the more she realized how stupid she'd been about Jeff. Maybe his father had gotten a call and a ransom note, the words made from letters cut from magazines, but two months was too long for a kidnapping to continue without a more aggressive request for money. The moment Uncle Nicky told her he'd tracked Jeff and the four robbers to the Bahamas, she should have been suspicious. She hated to admit how blind she'd been to what was going on. She'd had to be hit in the face with the truth before she believed it was not mere coincidence that her password had been used to get into the bank's system. How Jeff had managed it, she didn't know. Or why. Getting those answers was one more reason she wanted to get him back to the States.

Trevor slowed his pace as he neared the edge of the woods. Ahead of them was the village of Cayton and the airstrip. They'd crossed through the marsh without seeing any signs of Jeff or the others, but he had a feeling that was not a good omen. More than likely, the five were simply waiting for them to return. After all, where else could they go? The only way off the island was by plane or boat, and with a hurricane in the area, no sane person would be using either that night.

Of course, like his father, he'd always been considered a little crazy.

He was relieved to see the Navajo still sitting on the tarmac, exactly where he'd left it. He wasn't pleased to see his plane was still being guarded. Somehow Jana and he were going to have to get past that man and his rifle.

She came up beside him, and he motioned for silence with a finger to his lips. She nodded, saying nothing. She'd been quiet most of the way back, only grunting that time she tripped and gasping when he startled a frog and it jumped into the murky waters near her.

No more screams. Not that he blamed her for yelling out when she saw that iguana. On his first encounter with the island, he'd done his share of gasping and screaming.

Of course, being told by the locals that there was a dragon lurking in the reef and that three-fingered, three-toed, red-eyed gremlins lived in the woods hadn't helped. Now, instead of water dragons or chickcharnies, the monsters were living in the place he used to call home.

He knew that the house was sturdier than most of the shacks the locals lived in. His guess was that Jana's stepbrother and the others would wait out the storm right where they were and take off in his plane in the morning. In addition to the high winds, it was getting dark and flying by instruments would necessitate identifying themselves, something Trevor was sure they wouldn't want to do. That meant he had roughly ten hours to reclaim his airplane.

Jana moved, and Trevor glanced her way. She was walking off, following the edge of the woods as they'd done earlier that afternoon. He called after her, but the wind blew his words back in his face, and she kept going.

Taking off at a jog, he quickly caught up to her. He grabbed her shoulder, and she stopped and looked up at him. "Where are you going?" he asked.

"To get my stepbrother."

He shook his head. "You can't."

"I have to."

"With what?" He held up his hands. "Your bare hands?"

"If necessary."

"You're crazy." Except her calm, determined expression said she was anything but crazy.

She pointed at his plane. "Go ahead. Go save your

plane. Get out of here. I, however, am not leaving without my stepbrother."

"You'll be his prisoner in a minute."

"I'm already his prisoner. He's stolen my life. Even if I fail, I'm no worse off than I am now." Her expression softened, and she touched his arm. "I'm sorry. I shouldn't have involved you. Go ahead. Go."

"Not without you." He couldn't just leave her on her own on the island. Grabbing her arm, he began to pull her back toward the airstrip.

She planted her feet and resisted, her voice rising slightly. "I'll fight you, Trevor. Fight you all the way. How are you going to get your plane back and deal with me too?"

He pulled her gun from his pocket, deciding to use her tactics, but her expression didn't change. "Go ahead," she said. "Shoot. Don't you understand, Trevor? Unless Jeff clears my name, I'm dead."

Her cool acceptance frightened him. Gone was the neatly dressed, sweet-voiced sexpot who'd stepped into his office. In the gold-flecked green of her eyes, he saw a determination he knew he could not fight. He put the gun back in his pocket and released his hold on her arm. "Okay, go. Go get yourself killed."

For a moment she looked at him, neither condemnation nor exoneration in her expression, then she turned and walked away, her head held high and her back stiff.

He swore under his breath, watching her go, each step taking her farther from him. She was an innocent on the way to slaughter. Her stepbrother had set her up as the sacrificial lamb, only the lamb wasn't going to simply lie down and die. He admired her spirit, but what could she do? She was on an island she didn't know, alone with no one to help her.

He should let her go, he thought. She hadn't worried about him when she got him involved, hadn't considered his safety or what she was doing to his reputation. Like so many other pretty faces, she'd used him.

Used and discarded him.

He looked back at his plane. His future was tied up in that plane. He still owed a bundle on it and without it he had no business. He wouldn't even be able to collect the insurance on it, not if he told anyone it had been stolen while he was on an island that he shouldn't have been on according to his flight records.

In reality, there was no decision to make. Logically, he had to get his plane back. What else could he do? It was his livelihood.

Trevor took off at a slow jog, staying concealed by the trees. He caught up with Jana in seconds, once again stopping her. "All right," he said. "We get your stepbrother, then we get my plane. But we're going to need help."

She looked at him, and the relief and appreciation he read in her glance was enough to convince him he wasn't a total idiot. "What kind of help?" she asked.

"I have friends on this island. People who knew my father and kids I played with as a boy. Kids who are now grown men and women. Most of them are fishermen. They have flare guns on their boats. We need more than this pistol." He tapped the gun in his pocket.

"You think they'll give us their flare guns?"

"There's only one way to find out."

Jana ran her fingers through her hair as Trevor knocked on the door. Unlike the yellow house where her stepbrother was staying, this house had no pane-glass windows. Louvered glass slats covered all apertures, most now opened halfway because of the wind. Her reflection distorted, she couldn't really get a good look at herself, but she could imagine how she appeared. The makeup she'd so carefully applied that morning would be long gone, while the clothes she'd bought in the hopes of making her story more convincing hung limply on her body, not completely dry, ripped in places and dirty.

Each time she loosened a tangle of hair, the wind tore it from her touch, twisting it again. Through the partially open slats in the doorway, she saw a man approach. Before the door was even opened, Trevor called to him. "Guess what, man, you've got a fox on the island."

The door swung open. The man standing on the other side was not quite as tall as Trevor, nor as muscular, his grin wide and his teeth flashing a brilliant white against the mahogany of his skin. "Time to keep an eye on the hens, I think then." He glanced at Jana. "'Cept this time I see you brings your own."

"Or she brought me. Jana, meet Lynden Knowles, one of the best fishermen and liars on this island."

"Me lie?" Lynden opened his eyes wide, showing the white around the dark centers. "Nevha, man."

"And how big was that fish?" Trevor spread his hands wide.

"Big fish. Very big fish." Lynden grinned. "Come in, man."

Trevor motioned her to enter first, and she stepped into the wood-frame house. The interior decor was a mixture of old and new, store bought and handcrafted. The rugs were woven of palm fronds. The chairs looked like Salvation Army castoffs. Candles, lanterns, and battery-operated lamps sat on wooden boxes, and the walls were covered with religious artifacts, batik hangings, and colorful paintings. Jana recognized the oils as works by Trevor's father. There was a scene of a fishing boat, its nets hanging out to dry; a beach scape with frothy waves breaking on pink-white sand; and the portrait of a young black woman and a child, the little girl's eyes bright with excitement and her skin a soft shade of cocoa.

Jana found her gaze drawn to the child, then a movement off to her left pulled her attention away. A woman in her early twenties stepped into the room.

Pretty and slender, her skin a light cocoa brown and her eyes bright with excitement, she was wearing a colorful wraparound skirt and blouse. "You back," she said, her gaze locked on Trevor.

"Couldn't stay away," he responded, grinning and opening his arms wide.

She walked into his embrace, pressing her face against his chest and wrapping her arms around his sides. "I thought you never coming back."

He flinched, and she pulled back, looking at his right

side. "What this?" she asked, touching his shirt where the bullet had torn through the fabric.

"Just a little accident."

"Looks like—"

Trevor cut her off by turning toward Lynden. "This is a surprise. When did you and Tia get together?"

"Been some time now," Lynden said, grinning proudly as he walked into the room. "Wedding last March. We sent you invitation, man."

"You know how long it takes those mail boats to go from island to island. I'll probably get it next year."

Tia was still looking at his side. "Needs be cleaned."

Trevor turned back to Tia, brushed a fingertip over her cheek, then leaned forward and kissed her on her forehead. "Don't worry about it, honey. It's fine." Stepping back, away from her, he placed his hand on his chest. "It doesn't compare to the pain in my heart. How could you have forgotten me so quickly? Married this braggart?"

Jana watched the interplay between Trevor and the woman, feeling totally ignored and not liking or understanding the feelings of jealousy shooting through her. That Trevor had an old girlfriend on the island shouldn't surprise her. He probably had one in every port. Nothing about his personal life, past or present, should matter.

Yet for some reason, she cared.

As if finally remembering her, he looked her way. "Jana, this is Tia, the love of my life and the biggest pest around."

"Not pest." Tia gave Jana a suspicious look, then glanced back at Trevor. "She your woman now?"

Trevor smiled at Jana. "What do you say? Are you my woman now?"

"Your woman?" The idea was so ludicrous, she laughed. "No."

Once again, Trevor put on a pained expression. "I just can't win." Then he looked at Lynden. "What do you know about the people living where my father used to live?"

Tia spoke up first. "Bad men. Very bad men. One with glasses scares me."

Jana knew which one she meant. "That's my step-brother. He and the others robbed a bank. The bank where I worked."

"Ah." Lynden cocked his head as he looked at her, and Jana had a feeling he was beginning to understand why she and Trevor had come. He motioned toward the wicker and upholstered chairs in the living room. "Come. Sit down. Tell us about this robbery." He glanced Tia's way. "We have any beers?"

"Still have Kalik that Gaddy brings."

She started to walk out of the room, but Trevor called after her. "How about something to eat? I'm starved."

Tia looked back at him, and the coy, knowing smile returned. "You always hungry. I suppose the Fox wants chicken."

"Whatever you have."

"I bring Kalik, then fix food," Tia said, and left the room.

"Kalik is the beer of the Bahamas," Trevor explained to Jana. "It's not bad. Light. A little wheaty in taste."

Jana wasn't sure a beer, of any kind, would be wise as

hungry and tired as she felt. She wasn't a beer drinker and wasn't about to start. Besides, she didn't need to fall asleep in a drunken stupor, not when so much was at stake. Still she accepted the bottle Tia handed her when she returned, and she did take a sip.

She listened as Trevor told Lynden about the bank robbery. His brief summary was basically what she'd told him, and she didn't interrupt, but after a few minutes, she realized she had another need, one that surpassed the telling of her plight. "Do you have a bathroom?" she asked Lynden.

"Yes." He grinned. "My house has all modern conveniences. You look down hall." He pointed the way. "Second door to your right."

Jana excused herself and followed his directions. Modern conveniences, she discovered, meant an enzyme toilet and a gravity-fed water supply. As far as she could tell, the island had no electricity. The small room did have a mirror, and as soon as she'd relieved herself, she tried to repair the damage of wind and rain. Her reflection confirmed that her hair was a mess and her makeup gone, but those things seemed minor compared with her blouse. Trevor could have told her that she'd buttoned it wrong. Instead, he'd let her come to this house, let her sit and talk with these people—his friends—with one side totally askew from the other.

Quickly she rebuttoned her blouse and pushed the tail into her slacks. Feeling like a fool, she stepped back into the hallway. From there a savory aroma of simmering tomatoes and onions led her to the kitchen. Pausing in the doorway, she watched Tia add spices to a pot on the stove. Turning to reach for a knife, Tia saw her. For a moment, Tia stared at her, the look in her eyes suspicious, then she waved her into the room. "Come. This stew easy make. Be ready soon."

Cautiously, Jana entered the kitchen. On a chopping block was a fish, skinned and gutted but with the head still on, its glassy eye looking up at her. Tia severed the head with a quick chop of the knife, then proceeded to cut the remainder of the fish into chunks. Jana watched as Tia scraped all the chunks, the head included, into the pot on the stove.

"You like fish stew?" Tia asked, glancing her way.

"I think so." The fish head bobbed to the surface, a chunk of celery covering its mouth but its eye still staring toward the ceiling.

The sight bothered her, and Jana turned away and walked to the slatted window that looked out onto the road in front of the house. Through the partially opened glass, she felt the wind and could see the black clouds racing across the rapidly darkening sky. In the yard across the way, the fronds of a tall coconut palm, its trunk bent by the trade winds, snapped like whips.

"Bad storm coming," Tia said.

"You think we'll get more rain?" Jana faced her again. She'd hoped what they'd had earlier would be the extent of the storm. "What does the weatherman say?"

Tia smiled smugly. "Weatherman knows nothing. My mother says bad storm coming. Maybe as bad as hurricanes that come long time ago. When I little, my grandmother tells me about a storm she lives through, back in twenty-six. It so bad, she says, the water comes up into the house. People float by the doors."

Jana thought of Trevor's plane. The idea of its floating off was not one she wanted to consider. "Do you think this bad storm will hit tonight?"

"Maybe yes, maybe no. Storms, they have mind of their own. Come when they want . . . or not come." She grinned. "Much like men, yeah?"

"I guess," Jana said, wondering if Tia was talking about Trevor. Considering his behavior earlier that afternoon, she didn't think he would have any trouble coming when he wanted.

Not that she planned on finding out, one way or the other. What she needed to worry about was when the five men in the yellow house might decide to vacate an island about to be besieged by a hurricane. "How long have those men been living in Trevor's father's house?"

"More than a month now." Tia shook her head and went to the cupboard, getting down four bowls. "Since they come, I don't like to go out. One man, Steve, when he live here before, he bother me . . . pick fights with Lynden. Now I think other black man wants me. I don't like them. They scare me."

"They scare me too."

"My mother hear one say they waiting for it to cool down." Tia glanced toward the window. "Maybe this be cool enough for them. Then they go."

Trevor stepped into the kitchen, Lynden behind him. "You'll be pleased to know," Trevor said, "that Lynden has a plan that will help you."

SIX

An hour and a half later Trevor leaned against a wall in the living room and listened as Jana repeated her story of the bank robbery. In addition to him, her audience included five men and two women. The youngest was Tia and the oldest was Gaddy Rolle, who was pushing sixty. Tia's mother, Olive, who had grown more rotund since Trevor's father had painted the portrait on the wall, was probably in her fifties, while Lynden, Wally, Turk, and Joe were either Trevor's age or a couple years older. As a boy, he'd come to think of these people as his extended family. It didn't matter to him that their skin was dark or their manner of speaking different, though it always galled his mother when he returned in the fall to their house in upstate New York speaking English with the Bahamian dialect.

This evening, Olive and Gaddy had stopped by to see Tia and Lynden, as it seemed they often did, and had stayed for dinner. They now hung around out of curiosity. Lynden, on the other hand, had gone out after dinner and recruited the three younger men. Wally and Turk had been scrappers as boys, always into mischief or fights. They could be tough if necessary, though life in the Bahamas seldom required aggressiveness. Joe loved an adventure and would have been insulted if he'd been left out. Trevor only hoped the four of them understood this wouldn't be a lark. The men living in his father's old house were smart and dangerous. Their only mistake, as far as he could tell, was involving Jana. She was not one to give up without a fight.

He watched her lean forward in her chair, her hands moving as she spoke. *Italians talk with their hands*, he remembered Scarlotti saying. The slashing gesture Scarlotti had made across his throat the day he'd suggested what would happen if Trevor ever mentioned what he'd found in that cave had said volumes.

The way Jana spoke with her hands, however, was different from Scarlotti. Her gestures were graceful. Energetic. Beautiful.

Not that she wasn't determined. Trevor knew she meant it when she told the group that she was going to get her stepbrother into police custody, no matter what it took. Trevor himself was a casualty of her determination. And her analysis of the situation was on target. There were five men to be dealt with, one guarding the plane and four in the house. They were all armed and her stepbrother was not going to go with her willingly. This was not going to be a piece of cake.

Trevor appreciated her honesty with his friends. He

wished she'd been as honest with him that morning. *Why didn't you tell me?* he'd asked her earlier.

Would you have done it? she'd responded.

Hell no, he'd answered. He shouldn't even be helping her now. He should be using his friends to get his plane back, nothing more. Jana Jenkins meant nothing to him. Absolutely nothing.

Except she did.

It didn't make sense, but in barely twelve hours, he'd grown to care for her. Something about her triggered his protective urges . . . as well as other urges. From the very beginning, he'd been attracted to her, but his biggest mistake had occurred in the cave when he'd touched her.

There he'd discovered just how soft and smooth her skin was; had fallen under her spell when she responded to his kisses. How quickly she'd warmed to his touch. He could tell she was warm now, her cheeks rosy, and he would swear he caught a whiff of her perfume, the scent adding to her tantalizing allure.

The battery lamp on the orange crate next to her made her green eyes sparkle, and she kept running her fingers through her hair, pushing it back from her face. A nervous gesture, he was sure.

She made him nervous.

It would be so much easier if he could turn his back on her and walk out the door, but here he was, listening to her and planning ways to help her. Just give him a damsel in distress, and he bit: hook, line, and sinker. He'd been taken before, but this time the stakes were higher. This time he knew what he was getting into—the danger and the risk of failure.

"What we need are the flares from your boats," he said when Jana finished explaining the situation. "With them, and with your help, we can create a diversion. I don't want any of you getting close to the place, it's too dangerous, but Lynden came up with an idea that we think might work. If you guys shoot some flares by the house, the four men inside should come out to see what's up. And once they're outside, Jana and I can nab her stepbrother."

Gaddy was the first to speak. "Dis is not a good night for dis plan."

"We have to do it tonight," Trevor said. "Come morning, there's a good chance they'll take my plane and fly out of here."

Across the room, seated next to Tia, Olive shook her head. "Nobody leaving this island come morning. 'Cept, perhaps, if they is washed off."

"She feels it in her bones," Tia explained, looking at her mother. Olive nodded, the red bandanna wrapped around her head bobbing up and down, and Tia went on. "She says this storm's gonna be a big one—really big— and it's gonna hit tonight."

Jana looked at Trevor, as if expecting him to have an answer. Trevor wished he did. Considering the number of hurricanes that formed each year and how few ever actually hit Conch, he'd hoped this one would miss the island. He'd figured there'd be rain. Maybe a lot of rain. And wind. Some of the most recent gusts had already reached sixty to seventy miles an hour. But seventy-mile-an-hour winds were not hurricane winds.

The weatherman he'd been listening to that morning had compared this hurricane to the ones in '92 and '65. He'd been talking about winds of a hundred ten miles an hour or more. So far all they'd been getting was the fringe of the storm. If a hurricane with the intensity of Ned hit Conch, they would indeed be in trouble.

Trevor wished he could laugh at Olive's "feelings," but over the years he'd learned to trust her intuitions. If she said a big storm was going to hit, it was going to hit. What they had to do was plan for it; secure everything and anything that might be blown or washed away.

"My plane—" he said, a sinking sensation twisting through his gut as he remembered the two chocks he'd placed around the wheels. "My plane may not be there in the morning if the hurricane hits here."

Jana heard his fear and understood what Trevor was saying. His livelihood was in danger. If the hurricane was coming their way, he had to get his plane off the island and get it off fast.

She could feel her chances of nabbing Jeff slipping away, and knew she needed to think fast. "If we act right away," she said, using her hands to emphasize the need for speed, "we can have my stepbrother and be off this island before midnight."

She kept her gaze on Trevor, afraid he was going to opt for saving his plane and the heck with her and her stepbrother. He said nothing, simply stared at her.

One of the young men, Wally, stood and looked around the group. "What do you say, guys? Do we help her?" He turned to Trevor. "Ya gotta get that gunman away from your plane. Might as well get her stepbrother too."

Trevor's gaze never wavered from hers. "Might as well," he repeated with no enthusiasm.

She understood his reluctance and the irony. Just as her stepbrother had stolen her livelihood, she was doing the same to Trevor. How many wrongs made a right? she wondered.

"I'm gonna get my flares," Wally said, and started for the door. "And see if I can find my gun. Anyone else with me?"

"Why not?" Turk also rose. He winked at her, then glanced at Trevor. "Gotta help the pretty lady, right man?"

"Right," Trevor repeated. *Whether I want to or not*, his look said, and Jana glanced away, unable to face him feeling as guilty as she did.

Joe rose from his chair. "I've got fireworks," he said. "The noisy kind. Bought them for Junkanoo, but what the heck, might as well use them tonight."

All four of the younger men left to go to their boats or houses, while Olive and Gaddy stayed behind, along with Tia and Trevor. Jana stood and walked over to the window, hoping a little fresh air would help clear the queasy feeling in her stomach. She wasn't sure if the nausea was from nerves or from the fish stew, and she mentally kicked herself for taking more than two bites of that mixture. Two bites had been enough to tell her the spices were more than she was used to. Even worse was when Gaddy dished the fish head with its glassy eye into his bowl, then proceeded to eat it. Simply remembering that sight made her stomach turn. She gulped in another breath of fresh air and forced herself to think of something else.

"More beer?" Tia asked, bringing in a few bottles of the Kalik.

Jana turned down Tia's offer, but noticed Trevor took a bottle. Ever since he'd arrived, he'd been drinking. All of them had been drinking. Jana had no idea how potent the brew was, but she hoped she didn't end up with a bunch of drunks trying to pull this off. Her stomach turned again, and she knew fresh air wasn't going to help. Quickly, she headed for the bathroom.

Trevor followed Jana. He heard when she emptied her stomach and waited outside the bathroom until he was sure she was through. Then he stepped in, closing the door behind him.

She was on her feet, leaning against the basin Lynden had installed, her face as white as a sheet. "You okay?" he asked, knowing she wasn't.

"Yeah." She looked at him with glazed eyes.

He found a washcloth and wet it, then wiped her face clean. "Nerves will do that to you."

"I—I think it was the fish stew."

"If you say so." He pulled down a bottle of mouthwash and handed it to her.

She took a swig, rinsed her mouth, then spit it into the basin. "I'm not used to food that spicy," she said, straightening and handing the bottle back.

"Bahamian cooking is never bland."

"Would Tia try to poison me?"

"Tia? Poison you?" The idea caught him off guard. "Why do you think she might do that?"

"Jealousy. She loved you, you left her, and you came back here with me."

"And you think she would poison you to get me back?"

"Why not? You're a good-looking man." Jana smiled weakly. "If I were in love with you and you showed up with another woman, I'd probably do something irrational."

He chuckled. "I think you just might. Here I've just met you, and you've already done several irrational things. Hijacked my plane. Shot me."

"Oh, don't remind me." Her gaze dropped to his side and the tear in his shirt. "Have you looked at that?"

"It's fine."

"It's fine," she repeated, some of the color coming back into her cheeks.

She touched his shirt near the tear, and he didn't pull back. Watching her in the living room, he'd decided if they lived through this ordeal, he was going to lock her in a room and bawl her out.

Then he was going to make love to her.

Carefully, she lifted the edge of his shirt so the wound was exposed. He tried to keep his body relaxed, but the moment she looked up at him, her eyes filled with concern, he knew he'd never be relaxed around her. A simple look had him growing hard.

"It needs to be cleaned," she said.

"So clean it."

She licked her lips and stared at him, as if waiting for him to change his mind. He didn't. He wanted her to realize what she'd nearly done, and he wanted her hands on his body.

"How do I get hot water?"

"Cold will do." Hot water would require heating it on the stove and involving others. He wanted this between them.

"Cold," she repeated, and let go of his shirt. He pointed to the washcloths on a shelf, and while she got one, he unbuttoned his shirt, letting it fall to the floor.

She wet the cloth, then rubbed it over the bar of soap near the sink. When she turned back to him, he steeled himself for the first touch.

"This might hurt," she said, looking at his face, not the wound.

"It already hurts."

"Oh." She sucked in a breath, then tentatively touched his side with the wet cloth.

He also sucked in a breath, the cold almost as painful as the stinging of raw skin. He could tell she was being careful. Rather than rubbing, she patted the cloth over the area, turning it often to expose a clean spot until the whole cloth was tinged pink. Finally she turned back to the sink and rinsed out the washcloth. "I think it's clean now."

"Good." Although he had a fairly high tolerance for pain, he was glad she wouldn't be doing any more rubbing. The area was sore, even if it was more powder burn than actual wound.

As he watched her wring out the cloth, a crazy thought crossed his mind. "Now are you going to kiss it and make it better?"

The cloth dropped into the sink as she spun to face him. "Kiss it?"

"My mother always kissed the ouchie and made it better."

"I am not your mother."

"No, you're not." He grinned suggestively. "So a kiss on the lips will do."

She stepped back and away from him. "I don't think so."

He moved toward her, liking the idea more and more. "I think you owe it to me."

She shook her head and took another step back. "You got your kiss in that cave you took me to."

"That was to stop you from getting all hysterical on me."

"It was still a kiss." Her next step ran her into the wall. Wide-eyed, she looked around for a way to escape.

He closed the space between them, blocking all exits. "Afraid to kiss me?"

"Of course not." She lifted her chin boldly, looking him straight in the eyes. "What's there to be afraid of?"

"Exactly."

"I just wonder if this is something you really want to do, or if it's just because you've had so much to drink."

"I haven't had that much to drink." He combed his fingers through her hair, drawing it away from her face, then letting it fall back to her shoulders. "You have beautiful hair."

"Sure, all tangled and windblown." She caught his hands in hers. "Trevor, we hardly know each other."

"And I want to get to know you better." He cradled her face in his hands and tilted her head back even farther, then brought his mouth down on hers.

Jana thought of resisting, but only for a second. The moment Trevor's lips touched hers, she knew she wanted this kiss. Guilt and appreciation had been mingling within her for hours, and either could have been an excuse to kiss him, but she knew the truth. She could protest all she wanted, but she'd liked it when he kissed her earlier. Ever since then, the thought of being held by him, of feeling his arms around her and his hands on her body had been playing through her mind. The truth was, she'd been hoping he would kiss her again.

The whole idea was crazy. He was unpredictable, tainted by scandal, and totally different from the type of men she dated. She should be pushing him away.

Jana wrapped her arms around his neck and stepped closer.

She tasted the beer he'd been drinking and smelled it on his breath, but his actions were not those of a drunk. The steady assault he was waging said he knew exactly what he was doing to her. First he explored her lips, then invaded her mouth with his tongue, each thrust titillating her senses.

Her skin felt flushed, and she knew her insides were turning liquid. Slowly she let her hands slip down to press against his bare chest, her fingers brushing through a tangle of matted hairs. The contact of their bodies was intimate and tantalizing, conjuring up visions of naked lovers.

He moved away and she grabbed for him, not wanting the kiss to end. His chuckle was deep and knowing, but he abandoned her mouth and brushed her hair back from her face, giving him access to her neck. He nibbled on her earlobe, then trailed kisses down her throat. At the same time, she felt him slip a hand between them to release the top buttons of her blouse.

When he kissed the hollow between her throat and shoulder, then laved the area with his tongue, she groaned in pleasure and prayed her legs would hold her up. She wanted him to touch her breasts, to take off her clothes and touch her between her legs. She wanted to feel him inside her, filling her and exciting her. It was crazy, but she wanted him to make love to her right in this tiny bathroom where neither of them had space to move.

A knock on the door startled both of them. Trevor straightened, dropping his hand away from her blouse. "You two okay?" Tia asked from the other side of the door.

"Fine," Trevor said, his voice cracking. He looked at Jana and shook his head, smiling.

"Just fine," he said, the words coming out stronger this time.

"We getting worried," Tia responded.

"Jana wasn't feeling well. We'll—" He began buttoning her blouse back up again. "We'll be out in a minute."

He ran his fingers through her hair, brushing it back into place, then he kissed her on her forehead. "You go

on back with them," he said softly. "I need a few minutes."

She glanced down at the front of his chinos and understood what he meant. That he'd shared the same
thoughts she'd had was evident from the bulge beneath
his zipper. What had started as a simple kiss had gotten
way out of hand.

"Are—are you all right?" she asked.

He chuckled. "Frustrated as hell, but all right." He
nodded toward the door. "Go on. I'm going to look
around and see if Tia and Lynden have any salve or ban-
dages that I can put on my side. Tell them I had to take a
leak."

He opened the door and nearly pushed her into the
hall. Jana stumbled out, heard the door click behind her,
then looked to her side to see Tia standing only a few
feet away, watching her.

"He had to go," Jana said, feeling her face redden.

Tia turned away without a word and stepped back
into the living room. Jana sighed and followed her.

Olive was talking to Gaddy, and Tia sat down next to
her mother. Jana felt Tia watch every step she took across
the room, and the moment she sat down, Tia spoke.
"How long you know the Fox?"

"Not long," Jana answered. She looked at the others.
"He was helping me. I wasn't feeling well."

"But you better now," Olive said, her wide grin
showing her missing teeth. "You know why Trevor called
the Fox?"

"Because of his last name?" It made sense to Jana.

"Because he sly as the fox," Olive said. "And smart.

When he a boy, he goes into the woods, and the others they never find him."

"I could find him," Tia said, pouting.

"Because he let you." Olive patted her daughter's hand, the contrast in their skin colors dramatic. Dark chocolate and milk chocolate.

Jana saw Trevor step back into the room. He'd put his shirt on and had washed around the spot where she'd shot him. The frayed fabric now had a large wet spot darkening the check pattern.

Her gaze dropped to his slacks, and she smiled. Staying in the bathroom longer had worked; his chinos were loose across his hips. Not that she believed he'd forgotten what they'd just experienced. The way he was looking at her made her think more of a wolf than of a fox. A wolf quietly waiting and watching.

She didn't want him thinking she was grilling his friends about him and tried to explain why they were talking about him. "They wanted to tell me why they call you the Fox."

"Actually, what I would like to know," Tia said, looking at Trevor, "is how long the two of you have known each other?"

"It seems an eternity," Trevor answered, his gaze never leaving Jana. "We were introduced by a mutual friend. He knew I wouldn't be able to resist someone as pretty as Jana."

"She is very pretty," Olive said. "You two get married soon?"

"Oh, no." Jana didn't want them thinking this was more serious than it was. "We're . . . that is—"

"Just getting to know each other," Trevor finished for her.

"Wind's picking up," Gaddy said, cocking his head to the side.

The glass slats covering the windows rattled, and suddenly the door opened with a bang. Lynden came in, followed by Wally. "It's coming," Lynden said, and looked at Trevor. "I'm not sure you're going to have time to get this guy and fly out of here."

"Damn." He looked at Jana.

She closed her eyes and bit her lower lip, taking in a deep breath. Then she opened her eyes and looked at him. "You go," she said. "Save your plane. Save yourself."

"Not without you."

She shook her head.

"No," he said firmly. "I am not leaving you on this island. Maybe I couldn't have handled you and getting the plane back before, but I've got help now."

She glanced at Wally and Lynden, then back at him. "Why can't you just leave me?"

"Because, honey, you made me your partner, and I don't leave my partner."

"I don't want to be your partner." She stood and walked over to him. For a moment, she faced him, then turned toward the others. "You want to know how we met? Nicholas Scarlotti sent me to him. I met Trevor for the first time this morning. I tricked him into taking me up in his plane, then I pulled a gun on him and made him fly me here. After that, I shot him. That's our relationship. Now, help him get that plane back and get out of here. Make him understand, I'm not worth worrying about, that he needs to worry about himself."

The others looked at him, and Trevor shrugged. "Basically it happened like she said."

Joe came into the house then, breathing heavily as he dropped a canvas bag on the floor by Trevor's feet. "I got the fireworks," he said. "I also got some bad news."

"My plane's gone?" Trevor asked.

"No. Another plane here. Brings three men. Not American. Maybe Cuban. Maybe not."

"Maybe South American?" Jana and Trevor said in unison.

Joe shrugged. "Whatever, they not good. You know how there's a man guarding your plane? Well, he dead now. One of the three shot him. I saw it."

"It's Alvarez," Jana said, a tremor to her voice. "And his bodyguards, Carlos and Nardo." She looked at Trevor. "What do we do now?"

"You really planned this out well, didn't you?"

She sighed. "Trevor, I didn't plan any of this."

"Right on." He looked at the others. "Remember how we used to play soldiers? Ready to play again?"

"I think you need more dan four men," Gaddy said, pushing himself out of his chair. "I think maybe dis takes a whole village."

SEVEN

Time was of the essence. Gaddy outlined his plan, and the seven who lived on the island took off, leaving Jana and Trevor at the house to inventory the flares, guns, and fireworks the others had brought back. Within a half hour, the seven had returned, each having visited a half-dozen houses. Tia brought out colorful cloaks that she gave to Trevor and Jana, Olive painted white makeup on their faces, and Lynden found colorful feathers and hats. "Left over from last year's Junkanoo," he said.

"That's their version of Mardi Gras," Trevor explained to Jana.

Within an hour of the news that Senor Alvarez and his men were on the island, everyone was dressed for the festivities and the plan was ready to put into action. As a group they left the house, and Jana was amazed when she saw the crowd waiting outside. At least forty of the islanders, both men and women, were there, all dressed in brightly colored cloaks or vests, their faces painted, and headdresses adorning their heads. Some carried burning torches, the wind whipping the flames away from the tips, and others held flashlights.

At Gaddy's command, they gave a cheer and began moving toward the house on the beach that had once been Trevor's summer home. A singsong chant was started, a crazy mixture of English and Calypso that sounded vaguely familiar to Jana. Three men carried the beat on the steel drums they held, the tinny sound echoing ahead of them. Others picked up the rhythm in a swaying motion that was half dance, half walk.

It looked like a parade of islanders until the wind whipped Jana's cloak back, exposing the pale skin of her arms. Quickly she grabbed the edges of the material, pulling it closed. Olive pushed her toward the middle of the crowd, and others positioned themselves at her sides, sheltering her from view. Once again, the picture was of joyous abandon, but Jana felt the tension all around her. Those who had joined them understood the risk.

In her stomach, a new knot had formed, and Jana knew throwing up wouldn't make it go away. She twirled the noisemaker Tia had given her and swayed to the music, trying to blend into the party scene, but in her mind, she was going over the plan they had worked out before leaving Lynden's.

Jana knew they would only have a few minutes to pull off this caper. Everything depended on Jeff's coming out to see what was going on and not becoming suspicious. The most difficult part would be separating him from the others.

Wally and Turk split off from the crowd, scurrying to

the back of the house. Joe moved close to the veranda and kneeled to pull the fireworks from his bag. Jana knew that was her signal, and she looked for Trevor. He was already working his way toward the trees, taking a half-dozen islanders with him.

Trevor was in position when the flares, then the firecrackers, went off. Even with the wind, the noise was loud. To anyone who couldn't see the flares exploding in the sky, it would sound like gunfire, and Trevor tensed when the front door of the house flew open and Steve Romi rushed out, gun drawn. One thing Trevor didn't want was any of his friends being hurt.

The islanders sang louder, never missing a beat, dancing on the sand in front of the house and waving their torches at the waves breaking high on the shore.

Another series of firecrackers exploded, and Trevor saw Steve call back into the house. A moment later, there were three men standing on the veranda, then four as Jana's stepbrother joined them.

Steve yelled down at Joe, asking him what was going on. Trevor heard Joe's response. "We celebrating, man. Celebrating 'cause a storm comes."

"You're crazy," Steve yelled back.

Tia stepped out from the group and danced toward the house, waving to the men on the veranda and beckoning them to join her and the others. She headed straight for Steve, wiggling her body and smiling seductively, and Trevor wasn't surprised to see Steve shoulder his gun and start down the steps. Trevor remembered how Steve had always had the hots for Tia. And why not?

She was slender as a reed, beautiful, and tonight seemed to be offering herself to him.

Another of the younger women in the group danced toward the veranda, motioning for the others to come down. The two other robbers looked at each other, then at Jeff. Jeff said something that Trevor didn't catch, but from their expressions, he gathered the two didn't agree with Jeff's response. They shook their heads and started down the steps.

That left Jeff on the veranda. He stood by the steps, watching the crowd, the wind whipping his hair. *Come on*, Trevor thought, silently willing the nerdy looking man to move. *Come on down.*

Tia and the other young women pulled the three men into the crowd, dancing close and fully occupying their attention. Trevor knew the three would never know when they lost their guns. They would be thinking other thoughts when the women bumped up against them and ran their hands over their bodies.

Joe set off more firecrackers, and Jeff looked down at him. It was then that Trevor saw the others. The three men seemed to materialize out of the darkness, their pale complexions a distinct contrast to the dark-skinned islanders. Probably drawn by the noise, the three were looking at Jeff, but Jeff hadn't seen them. Trevor knew that the moment Jeff did, he would make a beeline for the door and the relative safety of the house. If they were going to get him before Alvarez did, it had to be now.

Trevor moved quickly, pulling off the headdress and cloak he was wearing and dashing from the edge of the woods to the house. Memories went with him, of times in the past when he'd run up those stairs ready to share some exciting news with his father. Now as he bounded up the steps, he watched Jana's stepbrother stare at him in surprise. It took a moment for Jeff to realize what was happening and turn toward the house.

Trevor hit him from behind, knocking him flat on his face on the veranda. He heard a thunk as Jeff's chin smacked solid wood, then a whizzing sound. Trevor wasn't sure if the sound came from a bullet passing by his head or from one of Joe's fireworks, but he crouched low and scooped up Jeff, swinging the dazed man over his shoulder. Staying crouched and using the house as a cover, he headed back for the woods.

He was glad Jana's stepbrother wasn't a big man; nevertheless, running against the wind with a semiconscious man draped over his shoulder was not an easy task. Too many years, he decided, had passed since his days in the marines. He was breathing hard by the time he reached the group with Jana.

"Go!" he yelled, hoping everyone remembered the second phase of the plan. "Go, now!"

The islanders moved away from them while Jana went with Trevor into the woods. She directed the beam of her flashlight on the ground ahead so he could see where he was going. The path was uneven, and he stumbled and tripped, but managed to keep his footing. His breathing labored, he headed toward the airstrip.

The next time he heard the whizzing sound, he had no doubt what it was. The bullet hit the tree to his left. The yelled warning came immediately afterward. "Stop!"

It was one word, but Trevor picked up the Spanish

accent. The South Americans were behind them. They'd fired a warning shot. No telling what they'd do the next time.

"Turn off the light," he ordered Jana.

The flashlight went off.

Trevor felt Jeff stir and eased the man to his feet. In the dark, he couldn't see Jeff's face, but he could tell the other man wasn't completely cognizant of what was going on. Under the circumstances, he didn't dare tell him. The sound of a voice would pinpoint their location.

"Give it up," another voice, clearly Hispanic, called into the darkness. "I know you are there, Senorita Jana. You and your thieving brother."

"Senor Alvarez, we can explain," Jana called back. "My stepbrother—"

The shot made a dull thud as it hit a tree off to Trevor's right. He heard Jana grunt, and an icy terror cut through him. A vision of her shot and bleeding and lying at the base of the tree galvanized him into action. Immediately, he let go of Jeff, shoving him aside, and started groping for Jana. Though he knew he was giving away his position, he called out her name.

"I'm okay," she answered from somewhere near his feet. "I dropped the flashlight and can't find it."

Crouching down, he found her. She felt soft and warm and very much alive. Quickly, he gathered her to him. "Forget the flashlight."

Another shot rang out, this one hitting the tree just above Trevor's head. He felt a hand on his leg, then a body bumped against his hip. "God, they're trying to kill us," Jeff whined as he crawled up beside them.

"I hear you," Alvarez shouted. "Either you tell me where my money is, or you are dead. All of you. I will show you to mess with an Alvarez. Nardo, where is Carlos?"

"Getting lights," Nardo yelled back, somewhere off to their left.

"Found it," Jana said, and Trevor heard a clicking sound, then her sigh. "It's broken."

Another shot hit the dirt not three feet from his side, and Trevor knew they couldn't simply stick around and wait for Alvarez to get his lights or a bullet to accidentally hit them. First he helped Jana to her feet, then he grabbed Jeff's arm, hauling him up and pushing him forward. Trevor had one goal in mind—to get them to the airstrip.

On a normal night, traveling through the pines and palms and madeira trees without a light would have been no problem for him. Moonlight and the stars had always given ample illumination when he was a boy. But there was no moonlight or stars tonight, only darkness and wind and the increasing sense of a ferocious storm about to hit.

Even after his eyes had adjusted, Trevor found it difficult to pick his way through the trees. Worse, he could hear Alvarez crashing through the underbrush behind them and knew once he had lights, the South American would have no trouble spotting them. There was no way they were going to escape, not if they stayed together. No way he was going to get to his plane.

Alone, he was sure, he would be fine. If he left Jana and her stepbrother, he could survive. And survival was the name of the game, wasn't it? That's what Lila had told him the day she came to visit him in the brig. She'd hung him up to dry and had saved her own skin. It was what Scarlotti had told him when he was sixteen. "You keep your mouth shut and you survive, and survival's the name of the game, kid. Remember that."

Trevor remembered.

Jana wasn't sure where Trevor was. She wasn't sure where anyone was, and she was afraid to call out. Keeping her hands outstretched in front of her, she inched her way forward, groping from tree to tree. Every step she took seemed to make noise, and though she could barely hear over the pounding of her heart and the roar of the wind, she was sure Alvarez knew exactly where she was headed.

She jumped as a loud bang reverberated through the air, and the sky became brilliant with light. Not sure she understood, Jana looked around. It was then she saw Alvarez and his bodyguard through the trees. The two of them were staring up at the sky.

Alvarez glanced down first, a half smile touching his lips when his gaze met hers. She watched, frozen, as he lifted his arm, pointing his gun directly at her. All hope of regaining her normal life zeroed in on the barrel of that gun, and she wondered if she would die instantly or if it would hurt.

She didn't hear the sound of the shot. It was the two hundred pounds hitting her side that captured her attention. In an instant her breath was knocked out of her and she was falling, her hip hitting the ground first, then her shoulder. She heard a grunt—Trevor's—and understood what had happened.

Just as quickly as they went down, Trevor was pulling her up. "Run," he said, dragging her to her feet and pushing her ahead. "Now. While we have light."

The flare's descent was nearly complete, the sky already growing darker. More shots rang out, and she ran, using what light was available to plan a route and sticking to it when it was once again dark. The headdress Lynden had given her fell off, then her cloak of colorful cloth snagged on a branch, and she tore it off, barely pausing before staggering on.

She heard a crashing noise behind her and had no idea if it was Trevor or Jeff or one of the South Americans. No idea where to go to escape. Everything she'd tried had failed.

Tears streamed down her cheeks, but she kept on running—stumbling and tripping, falling, and picking herself up again. Her shoulder hurt where she'd hit the ground, and a pain burned in her side. She stumbled again, fell, and half picked herself up.

Trevor nearly ran into her. If it hadn't been for a flash of lightning, he might have. But in that instant, he saw her standing directly in front of him. Sobbing.

The moment he touched her, she jumped. "It's me," he said loudly.

Though escape was important, he took her into his arms, holding her close and pressing her face against his chest as he rested his cheek against the top of her head. He knew her despair, could feel it in the shudders racking her body. Heard it in the half gulps of air she took in. Fear and adrenaline could only take you so far. She'd reached her limit, and so had he.

Another flash of lightning lit up the sky, and he glanced around. For the moment, at least, their pursuers were nowhere to be seen. Nor was her stepbrother. Trevor had a feeling Jana could forget about getting Jeff off the island. If Alvarez hadn't already killed him, he undoubtedly had captured him by now.

Exhausted or not, they couldn't stay where they were. The rain was coming down in earnest, the air growing cooler, and the wind picking up, so even the trees offered little protection. "We've got to keep going," he said.

"Going where?"

He heard the exhaustion in her voice, and the defeat. "We've got to find shelter. Somewhere where we can get away from this storm."

"That cave between the rocks?"

"No. I couldn't find it in the dark," he admitted. "But I know where there's another cave."

The storm had struck with a fury that surprised Jana. No longer were there simply gusts of high winds. Now they were being hit by a full-fledged gale. Every step she took was a battle, the trees around them creaking and groaning as they bent under the force of the wind. Limbs cracked and broke, flying dangerously through the air, and a torrent of rain beat down on them, soaking her clothes until the silk of her blouse clung to her like a second skin. The temperature plummeted, and she began shivering, her teeth chattering from a mixture of cold and fear.

All she wanted was to get away from the trees and falling branches, but once they came out of the woods, she wanted to go back. In front of her was nothing but ocean. Not the serene and idyllic ocean shown on posters of the Bahamas, but a wild and vicious sea riled to a frenzy by the hurricane.

They'd reached the edge of the island. Ahead of them was a drop-off of over a hundred feet, the waves beating at the limestone with a frightening fury. Trevor walked directly to the edge.

"This is going to be a little tricky," he yelled back to her. "But there is a path here that leads to a cave."

Jana stepped closer to his side, straining to see into the darkness. A flash of lightning gave her a momentary glance of where he wanted her to go, and her heart skipped a beat. What he called a path was no more than a few inches etched out of limestone and barely wide enough for her to place a foot. She wouldn't call it a sheer drop from the path down to the water, but it wasn't far from that. There was no way she could manage what he was asking.

"Come on." Trevor pulled on her hand.

She jerked her fingers free from his and shook her head, staring down at the waves licking up at her like a monster trying to devour its prey. Earlier, while putting on their costumes, he'd told her how the islanders some-times dressed up to scare off the water dragons lurking in the reef. The islanders were right. There were water dragons. She was facing one.

"It's not far," Trevor yelled. "I'll hold onto you."

He took her hand again, his fingers tightening around hers, but she drew little assurance from the gesture. The way the rain was coming down, she knew the limestone would be slippery. And if she slipped, she would pull him down with her. The dragon would have two to devour, not just one.

Again, she shook her head.

"We can't stay here," he said, leaning close to be heard. "And we can't go back."

She looked at the trees they'd just left, and as if reinforcing Trevor's statement, a pine fell under the onslaught of the wind, making a rending sound as its roots were torn from the ground.

Again, Trevor pulled on her hand.

If I'm going to die, Jana decided, *it might as well be with him.*

She'd gotten him into this mess. He had risked his life for her more than once in the last twelve hours. He was risking his life for her now. It seemed only right to follow him.

At her nod, he started. Pressing his body against the rocks, he inched his way along the face of the cliff, finding handholds with one hand and holding onto her hand with his other. The wind tried to peel them off, and each step was perilously slippery. The rain slid from her hair down her face, turning white as it washed off the makeup Olive had painted on. Jana couldn't breathe from fear and was sure she was going to pass out. Each minute seemed like an hour, and she wanted to ask how much farther, but was afraid. One misstep and he might slip. One break in his concentration and they were both goners.

She said a prayer, though she'd never considered herself religious. It had been years since she'd been to mass, years since she'd said confession. Still she mumbled the prayer as she crept along in the dark and hoped a power greater than she would give her absolution.

Lightning cracked, and she feared she'd said something wrong. Trevor's fingers tightened around hers, and she felt him slipping. He was moving rapidly downward. Falling.

Digging her fingers into the rock, she tried to hold on, then felt herself sliding along behind him.

EIGHT

As he let his body slide down the ledge, Trevor hoped he'd judged the distance correctly. The flash of lightning had only momentarily illuminated the entrance to the cave. Slightly below and in front of him, the opening resembled a gaping mouth in a wall of sea-etched limestone.

He thought he heard Jana scream as he pulled her with him, but he didn't dare look back. The difference between success and failure was only a few inches. He slid and skidded and wished he were as limber as he'd been at sixteen. Back then he'd scrambled along these cliffs like a mountain goat.

A gust of wind threatened to blow them both off the face of the cliff, and the rain was coming down so hard, it created a waterfall effect across the mouth of the cave. Ducking past a stalactite, Trevor cut through the water, bringing Jana with him. Another stroke of lightning gave him a view of the cave's interior, stalactites and stalag-mites, nesting birds and all. Then it was dark.

"Oh, my God," Jana said, stumbling to a stop beside him. "I thought we were goners."

"Not yet, but come on, we've got to move farther in." He took a cautious step forward. "We've got to get away from this wind and rain."

He relied on his memory of the cave's dimensions, along with the quick glimpses he got with each flash of lightning. The rain had soaked his clothes and water dripped from his hair down his face. With each step he took, his boots made squishing sounds, and he felt suddenly cold.

Another bright flash of lightning lit up the interior of the cave, and Jana stopped. He saw her shiver and stepped closer, wrapping his arms around her and drawing her tight against his body. "We made it."

"Do you . . . think anyone was following us?" she asked, her teeth chattering.

"No. And even if they were, unless they've seen this cave from the sea, they wouldn't know it was here. It took me four years before I discovered it."

"I was so scared." She wrapped her arms around him and snuggled her face against his chest. The delicate pressure warmed him from the inside out, and he rubbed his hands over her back, the wet silk of her blouse bunching beneath his palms.

A shift in the wind blew a fine mist of water into the cave. The spray touched the backs of his hands, and Trevor knew they couldn't stay where they were. "Come on," he said, and led her deeper into the darkness.

They worked their way around the hanging stalactites and past the stalagmites that rose from the floor of the cave until finally they found a wide sheltered spot among them. There Trevor sat, bringing Jana down with him and scooting her across his lap. Afraid she might not understand, he explained his actions. "This is a case of two bodies being warmer than one. Okay?"

She didn't object, but nestled closer, her teeth still chattering. "Do you . . . hear me . . . complaining?"

Once again, he rubbed his hands over her back in an effort to warm her. She continued shaking, and he drew her even closer, forcing her breasts to flatten against his chest. He had little heat to give, but he wanted her to have it all.

She shifted her weight on his lap, and he suddenly realized the dangers of the position. As her bottom wiggled across his hips and her chest rubbed his, nipples hardened by the cold poking at him, he felt an instinctive reaction. One muscle in his body distinctly hardened as his internal thermostat rose, and he knew Jana could feel his reaction. That she wiggled even more didn't help.

"I don't know about you," she said, "but I'm wet."

"Sorry, but I didn't see any clothes dryers in here."

He wasn't quite sure what she was doing when she slipped a hand between them and moved her fingers. However, when she touched his throat with her lips, her tongue darting in and out to play over his skin, he knew that the tingle running through him had nothing to do with a chill.

"What are you—?" he started, but didn't finish. She was kissing his neck, blowing her breath over the stubble of beard covering his chin, and again her fingers wiggled, then moved lower, her knuckles pressing into his chest.

"I'll give you all night to stop that," he said, searching for a little levity.

He needed to laugh, to remember where they were and what was happening. Instead, he groaned and stroked his hands over her back. She felt soft and feminine and smelled sweetly desirable. He liked her spirit and he liked her body, and they were just too close for him to keep a clear mind. He tangled his fingers in her hair, squeezing water from the wet tresses, then slowly drew her head back.

For a moment, he paused, waiting for her protest. A rumble of thunder was the only complaint he heard and another strike of lightning gave him a glimpse of her face.

She was not going to protest.

In her eyes, he saw desire, naked and undisguised. She wanted him as he wanted her.

He found her lips and claimed them. Not gently or tentatively, but with a thrust of his tongue that announced his desire. His need was primitive, fed by the feel of her body and a passion that had been growing from the moment he'd first laid eyes on her. That she didn't pull away but moved her mouth with his, the tip of her tongue coming into play, only added to his hunger for her.

He knew what she'd been doing with her hand as soon as she wiggled out of her blouse, the buttons undone. "Take off my bra and your shirt," she whispered near his ear. "We'll be warmer without them."

He willingly complied, finding the clasp of her bra and releasing it. She was naked to the waist, her skin damp and cool, and he leaned back and jerked off his shirt, tossing it aside. Once again he drew her close, and he sighed as her hardened nipples touched his skin. His body, already sensitized by the cold, turned every movement she made into a combination of ecstasy and torture. Holding her close, he massaged her shoulders, then her back. What was cold grew warm, both friction and desire fueling the heat.

Jana closed her eyes, savoring the growing warmth and the sheer masculinity of Trevor's body. He was right; two bodies were warmer than one, especially the way her body was reacting. Sitting on his lap, feeling the hardened pressure beneath her hip, she'd decided to take his theory a step further. It held to reason if they got out of their wet clothes, they would be even warmer. And if they made love . . .

The hairs on his chest caressed and tickled her while his day's growth of beard scratched her face. With each kiss, her mind grew more clouded. She knew what she was doing wasn't logical, but it didn't seem to matter. Nothing mattered anymore. Her life was a mess, and finding warmth through pleasure seemed the sanest thing in the world to do.

She ran her hand along his side, working her way down his ribs until she came to the wet material of his trousers. Her insides trembling with anticipation, she pressed her palm against his hip, then shifted her weight so she could slide her hand between their bodies.

She heard his intake of breath when she touched him, then his uncertainty when he said her name. "Jana?"

He grew even harder beneath the touch of her fingers, and she wished she could see his expression. "Yes?"

"Are you sure you know what you're doing?"

The husky quality of his voice made her sure. Perhaps this was only lust, but he wanted her. At the moment, she needed that. "Make love to me, Trevor," she said. "Please."

She felt a shudder run through him, but he said nothing. His silence made her fear she'd gone too far, and embarrassment swept over her. She started to remove her hand, but he caught it, his fingers engulfing hers. "You're sure?"

"I'm not sure of anything anymore."

"I don't have any condoms with me."

She laughed at the idea. "Trevor, we're not going to live long enough to have to worry about that. We're not going to get off this island. Either Alvarez is going to kill us, or the hurricane . . . or the cold."

"Not if I can help it, honey."

"Yeah. Right."

"You don't believe me, do you?"

She believed he would try. "I want to believe you. Look, if you don't want to—"

He cut her off. "Honey, I've wanted to make love with you from the moment I first saw you."

She'd played on that desire, had used it to trick him. Knowing her efforts had worked didn't ease her guilt. "Maybe this is a bad idea."

"Maybe it's a great idea." He moved, bending to the side, and she heard him pat the ground. "It's not going to be the softest bed."

She also reached down and touched the flooring of the cave. It was bumpy and gravelly, a mixture of uneven ridges and crumbled limestone. "It will be fine."

He brushed a spot smooth, creating a bed for them, and gently laid her on it. She said nothing as he finished undressing her. She was afraid if she spoke, he would know how nervous she was. Her body was tense, every nerve ending tingling. He brushed a fingertip across the fine hairs between her legs, and she sucked in a breath.

Never in her life had she made love with a stranger. Not that she hadn't had the opportunity. As the customer service representative at the bank, she'd come in contact with a lot of men—rich men and good-looking men— who'd not only opened an account, but also had openly propositioned her. She'd never been tempted, though. Long ago, she'd made a vow to herself. No going out with men she didn't know, and no making love until she was certain it was safe. It was only logical in this day and age.

But she wasn't a customer service representative any more, and never would be again, and logic had vanished from her life, along with safety and security. Lying naked in a cave with a man she barely knew seemed ironically appropriate.

In the darkness, she groped, finding his shoulders and holding onto him. He kissed her left breast, his whiskers scraping against her skin. Her hands slid up to his hair, still wet and clinging to his head. When he switched his kisses to her right breast, erotic sensations tingled through her, and she writhed beneath him. She bumped her leg against his shaft, its warmth and hardness stunning her into stillness. She hadn't even realized he'd taken off his pants.

She heard him chuckle, the deep rumble arousing, and he lowered his hips, rubbing himself against her, teasing her. "You know what I'm finding out about you?" he said, his lips only inches from her ear.

"What?" she asked, her breathless voice revealing her tension.

"You, my dear, only plan things so far."

"Not so," she rasped, knots twisting in her stomach as he enticed her with a gentle prod.

"You certainly didn't have much of a plan when you hijacked my plane."

"I needed . . . to get to this island. That was my— my plan. Trevor?" His hands had moved down between her legs, the touch of his fingertips scattering her thoughts.

He ignored the question in his name. "And once you got to this island? What was your plan then?"

"I told you . . . I . . ." She sucked in a breath. He had lowered his head, creating a trail of kisses that traveled downward. Down to where his hands were tantalizing her. "Trevor?"

He spread her legs and kissed her, and she couldn't catch her breath. His tongue teased her, finding just the right spot, and she knew if she didn't stop him, she was going to climax.

Placing her hands on his head, she pushed him away. "No. Don't. You can't . . . "

He leaned back just slightly. "Can't? You have done this before, haven't you? Made love, that is? You're not a virgin, are you?"

"No, I'm not a virgin." She was quivering inside. "It's just . . . I've never—"

"Never what?"

"You know." She wasn't going to explain. "Been kissed the way you were kissing me. Where you were kissing me."

"And do you dislike being kissed there?"

"I . . . It's just . . ."

Again, he chuckled, then he stretched himself over her like a blanket, holding himself up so his weight was a warming pressure, not a burden. "Your body feels warmer, but you're still trembling."

It wasn't from the cold. "I'm fine."

"Hmm, you're better than fine." He nuzzled her neck. "I like you, Jana Jenkins, or whatever your name is. You have a pretty face." He caressed the sides of her face. "A nice body." His hands moved lower. "A passion for life."

She laughed self-consciously, aware of her scent on him. "Lately it's been a passion for getting into trouble. I can't believe what I've done in the last two months."

He nibbled at her earlobe. "And what were you like before?"

She could hardly remember. "Conventional. I had a steady job, a steady boyfriend."

Trevor stopped nibbling. "And where is this steady boyfriend now?"

"Gone."

"Gone where?"

She hesitated, wondering herself. "Who knows?" It seemed laughable. "I'm certainly not conventional now. No steady job. No steady boyfriend. No life."

"So what was his name?"

"His name?" For a moment, she'd forgotten. "Phil. Phillip W. Bangor. He was a man 'on the fast track to success.' Those were his words. On his way up the corporate ladder."

"Were you engaged?"

"We'd talked about marriage, but I didn't have a ring. I think Phil was glad about that. It made it easier for him. Funny how distant a guy can get when you're accused of robbing a bank, especially when it comes out that your father was a member of the Mafia."

"Do you still love him?"

Jana thought about the word before she answered. "No. Love has a way of disintegrating when it's not coupled with loyalty. I cried when he left, but now that I look back, I think they were tears of disappointment, nothing more."

She felt the tears again, welling in her eyes. "What is this?" she asked, needing to change the subject. "You're asking me about past lovers while lying naked on top of me? I think I've lost my touch."

"Oh, your touch is fine." He ran his fingertips along her cheek. "I just don't want you regretting this when we get back to the States."

"You're assuming we will get back." She reached up and touched his face, wishing she could see him better. "I'm sorry, Trevor. It was selfish of me to involve you in this, even if I did believe you were running drugs. Uncle Nicky said—"

He cut her off with a laugh. "Good ol' Uncle Nicky. See this cave?" He shifted position on top of her, leaning more to one side. "This is where I found his stash of cocaine. Right back there." She had a feeling he was pointing, but she couldn't see. "Probably a million dollars worth. Maybe more. I never did tell anyone, and this is the first time I've set foot in here since that day."

Jana wasn't sure what to say. "I never knew he was into drugs. Oh, maybe subconsciously I knew he might be. That's probably why I believed him when he said you were being watched by the DEA and were scum and deserved anything that happened to you."

"Do remind me to thank him."

"You could have been shot—"

"I was shot," Trevor said coldly. "By you."

She touched his side, feeling the bandage he'd put on earlier. She wanted to forget that moment. "You know what I mean. Tonight, in the woods. I thought I was going to be killed when Alvarez pointed his gun at me. Then out of nowhere, you came to my rescue. You probably saved my life, but you risked your own."

"I have a habit of getting myself into these kinds of fixes."

"Which in turn gets you in trouble with the law." She was beginning to understand. "You won't be in trouble this time, will you?"

"You mean after they have my hide and throw me in prison for the rest of my life?" He scoffed. "Honey, I might not be guilty of running drugs, but the U.S. government frowns on pilots flying across the ADIZ without clearance, especially when that pilot is carrying a passenger who happens to be a robbery suspect and wanted by the police. If we get off this island alive, I might as well toss my license."

He sighed and levered himself off her. "If you'll excuse me."

"Where are you going?" she asked as he walked away. The absence of his body left her feeling cold and lonely, and she sat up herself.

"I've kind of lost my inclination to make love and nature calls," he said, and the next flash of lightning silhouetted his body near the mouth of the cave.

Jana sighed. Leave it to her to mess up a seduction. It seemed she could do nothing right.

Maybe she shouldn't have watched, but she did. Perhaps because she was afraid Trevor might suddenly disappear, leaving her totally alone. Or maybe because she found him so different from other men she'd known, she wanted to learn everything about him.

Trevor was totally different from Phil, both physically and in personality. Phil couldn't have carried her stepbrother from the house to the woods, couldn't have outrun gunmen or descended a cliff. And Phil wouldn't have kissed her as Trevor had, wouldn't have thought it proper.

Erratic spears of lightning showed Trevor walking back to her. Uncle Nicky had sent her to Trevor, had planted the idea in her head that using him would be all right, could be justified because of his past. They were all pawns, all suckers.

She said nothing when he sat beside her. He spoke first. "Wind's really blowing out there. Harder than before."

"How long do you think this will last?"

"Who knows. We might as well try to get some sleep."

She knew she'd have to answer nature's call herself before she could sleep. "You didn't happen to see a toilet when you were up front, did you?"

"Just go near the entrance. The way that rain is blowing in, everything will be washed away."

"Promise not to look?"

"And did you look?"

"With a man, it's different. You had your back to me. I couldn't see anything. It's not quite that easy for a woman."

He chuckled. "Okay, I promise I won't look, and I'm sure the birds won't tell."

She'd forgotten about the birds nested up front. "Do you think there's anything else in this cave with us?"

"The last time I was here, there were bats farther back, where it's darker. I think I still smell them. And I'm sure there are spiders."

"I think I wish I hadn't asked." She reluctantly pushed herself to her feet and made her way to the entrance of the cave.

Trevor did watch for a while, just to make sure she made it to the entrance without any trouble. Each streak of lightning gave him a teasing view of her body, and once again the idea of making love with her played through his thoughts. Talking about the trouble that lay ahead had killed his feelings of desire, but what the heck, if he was going to lose everything, he might as well enjoy himself while he could.

He found her fascinating. Fascinating, beautiful, and stubborn.

That he felt protective toward Jana was crazy, but he couldn't escape the feeling. No more than he could say she meant nothing to him, for if that were true, he would have taken off when he could, would have left her long ago. Somewhere between the Florida coast and Conch Island, he'd gotten involved with her, like it or not. Now the question was, how involved was he?

He heard her coming nearer, then her foot hit his. He found her hand and guided her down beside him. "Better?"

"Better."

"All ready for beddy-bye?"

She hesitated a moment. "Should we put our clothes back on?"

"They're still wet."

"Right."

"If we lie next to each other, we'll stay warm." He eased her down, stretching out beside her and cuddling close so her backside fit inside the curve of his front. "How's that?" He draped one arm over her front, cupping a breast in his hand.

"Trevor?"

"I'm only trying to keep you warm." Nevertheless, he

felt himself growing hard against her back and knew she also felt it.

"I want you to know," she said softly, "that I do appreciate everything you've done."

"That's good." He kissed the nape of her neck. Her hair was drying, becoming fluffy, and he blew a tress to the side.

"Do—do you think your friends are all right?" she asked.

"I hope so."

"I have a feeling Alvarez got Jeff."

"I wouldn't be surprised."

"He'll kill him, you know."

Trevor kissed another spot on her neck. "And how do you feel about that?"

"At the moment, I don't care."

Her breathing was becoming shallow. He laughed softly. "Warming up?"

"Oh yes."

"I think we'd better get some sleep."

"Whatever you say."

He felt her breast growing firmer, her nipple rising to touch his palm. A part of his anatomy was also growing firmer. Gently, he turned her toward him. "On the other hand, I think sleep can wait."

NINE

Trevor kissed her, and Jana found pleasure in the familiarity of his lips. It seemed impossible that in such a short time she'd become addicted to the taste and feel of him, but one kiss only made her want more. The thrust of his tongue was matched by hers as she explored and discovered.

"Touch me," he said, and she did, learning his body as he learned hers.

She found coarse hairs and sinewy muscles and heard him groan and suck in a breath when she stroked lower, wrapping her fingers around the hard shaft of his arousal. He was man, and she was woman. Their differences excited her. She rubbed him, delighting in the way he tensed. All too quickly, he put his hand over hers.

"You keep that up," he said, "and this is going to be over before we start. Slowly. We need to take this slowly."

They tried, but like a spark amid tinder, the passion

flared until the fire blazing between them engulfed them, and they were both hot and sweaty. For Jana, everything they did was new and exciting. Making love with Trevor was unpredictable and impetuous. Liberating.

Outside the cave, the hurricane vented its forces. Inside, they created a storm of their own. She was caught in a torrent of emotions, the warmth of his breath blowing over her skin and the touch of his fingers turning her insides wet. He teased her until she begged for relief and two became one. After that, all reality disappeared.

For her, what few vestiges of civilized behavior remained vanished. She twisted and bucked beneath him, tearing at his back with her nails. His need became hers, and together they soared and became a part of the storm. Together they kept it going until she was sure she would die from sheer pleasure.

The moment she climaxed, she knew it had never been this good or this earth shattering. Hearing him cry out his release only added to her satisfaction. Never again would she be content with men like Phil. For a moment in time, she'd experienced pure ecstasy.

Trevor eased himself off her, settling by her side and cuddling her close. A sigh of contentment was all he gave, and she didn't dare speak. Her thoughts were too chaotic, the heat still burning through her veins, and her body limp and exhausted. One word teased her mind with its impossibility.

Love.

Even as she thought it, she knew the idea that she might be falling in love with Trevor Fox was crazy. A person didn't fall in love like this. Love was something that grew over time. She barely knew him. Love was when two kindred souls came together. She had nothing in common with Trevor.

Nestled in the curve of his body, she tried to rationalize her feelings. She was mixing up a little lust with something that went much deeper. She was confusing an emotional release with an emotional bonding. What she was feeling couldn't be love.

It just couldn't be.

Yet if it wasn't, why was she grinning like an idiot and feeling all warm and loving?

She touched the arm he had draped over her side, and he stirred and sighed. Silently, Jana laughed at herself. Here she was analyzing what had happened and how she felt, and Trevor was asleep. How like a man. And how foolish of her to even connect the word *love* with what they'd just experienced.

It was lust, all right. Or maybe a crazy way of combating fear. She'd certainly had her fill of fear that night. It didn't even matter what she called it since she was either going to die or spend the rest of her life in prison. Nothing mattered, she told herself, her eyelids growing heavy. Nothing at all.

Nevertheless, as she drifted off to sleep, somewhere in the back of her mind, Jana wondered if she could be in love with Trevor Fox.

Trevor woke to a gray haze, and for a moment lay where he was, trying to bring his thoughts into focus. Sometime during the night, Jana had turned so she now had a leg draped over his and a hand pressed against his chest. Though they were still both naked, her body was as warm as his. He inhaled the scent of her and listened to her soft, rhythmic breathing.

He'd known making love with her would be good. The way she moved when she walked and the way she'd responded to his kisses had hinted at how she'd make love. But in truth, he hadn't been prepared for how responsive she would be, or how it would affect him. In his thirty-two years, he'd made love to many women, some experienced and others shyly naive. He'd even thought he was in love a couple of times, the emotion getting him into more trouble than he needed.

But that had been years ago. Now he couldn't remember how long it had been since he'd been with a woman. Maybe a month. Maybe two or three. He hated to admit it, but his love life had been in the pits for way too long.

Abstinence, he decided, was not good for a man. It made him think crazy thoughts. Made him think he cared about a woman he barely knew.

Don't get involved, he told himself. *Don't be a fool.* Experience should have taught him something by now. He knew what would happen once they got off the island, and he was determined they would get off the island. Jana Jenkins would be out of his life faster than a rat deserting a sinking ship. To believe anything else would be idiotic.

She stirred beside him, her fingers trailing down his chest, and he felt his body respond. The desire to make love with her was still there, even stronger than before, now that he knew how good it would be.

His father used to tell him that life wasn't fair. At the moment, Trevor fully agreed. It wasn't fair that Jana had popped into his life like this, that he cared what happened to her, or that she made him feel so good. It wasn't fair that she would leave him as easily as she had come, and that he would have only these memories.

He knew mentally tormenting himself would not change the way things were, and lying beside her, wanting her, was going to drive him crazy. He gently pushed himself back, easing out from under her leg and sliding her hand off his chest. Standing, he brushed the loose limestone from his body, flexed his shoulders, then walked toward the entrance to the cave.

Most of the birds that had been nesting there the night before were gone. The few left startled as he neared and rapidly flew out of the cave. The rain had stopped, the sky was a brilliant blue, and only an occasional drip of water, randomly falling from the ledge above the entrance, remained as a reminder of the storm.

Trevor stepped out into the sunshine, unconcerned by his lack of clothing. Below him the sea was still a turbulent mass of foam and waves, churning its fury against the coral and rocks. No fishermen would be going out on the sea today. From the quietness of the air and the bank of clouds in the distance, he knew what was happening. The storm wasn't over; this was merely a respite. The eye of the hurricane was passing over, and in a while the rain and the winds would return, lashing out at everything and anything in their path.

He turned and stepped back into the grayness of the cave, taking a closer look at his surroundings. It seemed like only yesterday, not sixteen years ago, that he'd walked into this cave for the first time, so excited by his discovery. How quickly that excitement had turned to fear.

Today there were no bales of cocaine stashed behind stalagmites, hidden from the authorities until it was time for them to be transported to their destination. There was no Nicholas Scarlotti to threaten his life. Birds' nests and a few spider webs were all he saw . . . and Jana.

She was sitting up, her blouse back on, the wrinkled and damp silk no longer chic and simply knotted in front rather than buttoned. She had also slipped on her panties. She glanced away the moment he looked at her. When she spoke, it was to a spot on the cave's floor. "What's it like out there?"

"Quiet right now, but we're not out of it. This is just the eye of the storm."

She still didn't look at him. "Think we should try to get back to your plane?"

"No. Even if we succeeded, there's no way I could fly off this island now. We'd be flying right into the storm." He didn't add that he wasn't even sure there was a plane to go back to.

"So what do we do?"

"Wait."

She seemed nervous about that and glanced around, but still she would not look directly at him. "I don't imagine there's any food stashed in here," she said.

"Not unless you want to nibble on a spider or two."

He saw her shudder. "No thanks. That might be as bad as trying to keep down that stew with the fish head."

"We've got to toughen you up a little." He went over to where he'd tossed his trousers and dug into a side pocket, pulling out two candy bars. "Here, Tia gave me these." He grinned. "Well, actually, I stole them from her, but she's used to that."

"Thanks." Jana gave him the quickest of glances, took one candy bar, and began peeling off the wrapper.

"Take both," he urged, holding the second candy bar toward her. He'd eaten two helpings of the fish stew the night before and was used to going without a meal or two. Jana, on the other hand, appeared tired and wan.

She looked at the candy bar he held, and he knew she wanted it. "Got to keep up your strength," he said. "You had a rather hectic night."

The moment he said the words, a blush of color rose to her cheeks. Although she took the second candy bar, she lowered her eyes, concentrating on the candy as if two bars of chocolate were an epicurean treat. Her behavior seemed strange until he glanced down at himself. The sight of her had given his anatomy a slight lift. He was proudly announcing to anyone who cared that he was interested in more than breakfast and conversation.

Realizing it was his physical condition and lack of clothing that bothered her, he again picked up his trousers. They were still soaked. Smiling, he spread them out on a rock, then lay his shirt and his underwear next to them. It looked as though Jana Jenkins was just going to have to get used to seeing him naked. At least for a while longer.

"I hope it will warm up a little," he said. "And our clothes will dry out. I'm not into wash and wear."

He sat beside her, but she kept her head turned so she was looking straight ahead. "At least it's not as cold as it was last night," she said. "It's almost balmy right now."

"Almost. Daylight puts a different slant on things, doesn't it?"

She cocked him a glance.

"Sorry you made love with me?"

Again, she looked forward. "No." She swallowed hard. "I just . . . Well . . . Aren't you going to put any clothes on? Your underpants or something?"

Trevor chuckled. "I take it Phillip didn't run around naked."

"He was rather conservative."

"And so are you, right?"

She blew out a breath and finally looked at him. "I used to be." Tentatively, she smiled. "I used to be a lot of things I'm not anymore."

"If you tell me you used to plan things, I'm not going to believe you."

"I did have a day planner. I even planned on coming to the Bahamas someday. I was going to lie on the beach, sip exotic rum drinks, and spend my nights gambling at the casinos."

"Not being shot at, dashing through the woods, and making love in a cave."

She shook her head. "That wasn't on my agenda."

"Look at it this way. Think of all you can tell your grandchildren."

"If I live to have grandchildren."

"You'll live." He slipped an arm around her shoulders

and gave her a reassuring squeeze. She flinched, and he eased his hold. "What's the matter?"

"I think I bruised my shoulder when you tackled me last night."

"While we were making love?"

"No, when Alvarez was aiming his gun at me. I hit my hip and my shoulder." She glanced down at her hip.

"Ah yes, Alvarez."

"Personally, I wish this hurricane would blow away my stepbrother, Alvarez, and all the others." She pulled her knees to her chin, wrapping her arms around them, and sighed. "What brought your father to Conch Island?"

"The solitude. My father was a man who liked to be alone. Why he ever married my mother, I'll never know. They were as opposite as they come. She wanted to mingle with society, be in the 'in' crowd. All he wanted to do was paint. That they stayed together for nine years was probably a miracle. Actually, the divorce worked out best for both of them. My father inherited some money when his parents died. Mom got most of it in the divorce settlement and was able to mingle with the 'in' crowd in our small town. Dad had enough to travel and found Conch Island. Once he started painting the islanders and his surroundings, his paintings sold and he never had to worry about money again. And since he sent some to Mom, neither did she."

"You spent every summer here with him?"

"Starting when I was twelve until I joined the marines. When I was young, Mom didn't like it. Every summer she was sure I'd come back a savage, but she knew if she refused to let me come, Dad would stop sending her money. So I came here as soon as school let out and returned to upstate New York and Mom just before school resumed."

"And did you return a savage?"

"In her opinion, yes. Every August my skin would be almost as dark as Tia's, and I was talking like an islander."

"You seem very close to Tia," Jana said cautiously. "I assume you and she—" She hesitated. "That is, was there, ah . . . something between you once?"

Trevor chuckled. "Once and forever. Actually, Tia and I think there's a lot between us, but we don't know for sure." When Jana glanced at him, he explained. "I think Tia is my half sister. We know that before I ever came here my father and Olive spent some time together. Then my father went away for a while—back to the States—and when he came back, Olive had married Gaddy Rolle and was about to give birth to a baby.

"Considering how light Tia's skin coloring is and how affectionate my father always was toward her, she and I are pretty sure we're half sister and brother. But Olive won't admit it and neither would my father. Why? Were you jealous?"

"Me?" Jana tried to look surprised by the question. "Why would I be jealous? I barely know you."

"We did make love last night."

Quickly she looked away. There was something she needed to explain. "About last night . . ."

"What about it?"

"That really isn't something I usually do. That is,

make love with a man I've just met. And I don't usually yell out like that. I don't know what got into me."

He grinned mischievously. "I did."

That he could joke about it and she couldn't, bothered her. "I mean—"

"Don't try to analyze it, Jana." He reached over and touched her chin, running his thumb along her jawline. "It happened. And I think you'll agree with me, it was pretty special."

She was glad to hear he thought it was special. "It—it was different." She licked her lips, her gaze traveling over his face. "I . . . ah, I really never have acted that way before." Remembering how she had acted, she pushed him forward so she could see his back. "Oh, dear." Gently, she touched the red welts where she'd scratched him with her nails. "I'm sorry. I didn't mean to do that."

He chuckled. "You were a wild woman."

Crazy better described her, she thought. "Back in Florida, do you . . . ah, have a girlfriend?" She hoped the question sounded casual. "I mean, I'd hate to have you trying to explain these scratches to another woman if we do get off this island."

"*When.*" He emphasized the word. "*When* we get off this island. And no, there is no one I'm going to have to explain anything to."

She was glad but tried not to show it. "I imagine it was fear that made me act that way last night. I mean, you and I, well—" She laughed, but instead of its sounding lighthearted, it came out stilted.

"Last night, I thought you and I made quite a pair."

The soft tone of his voice caressed her, and when he ran his fingers through her hair, she looked at him, then wished she hadn't. A woman could get lost in eyes that blue. She fought for sanity. "Trevor, we hardly know each other."

"We know more about each other than most people who met twenty-four hours ago."

She felt a flush of heat in her cheeks and looked away, afraid if she didn't, she might let her gaze slip down to his hips. If only he'd put on some clothes. Just his briefs would help. There was something very disconcerting about talking to a man in the buff.

"So what do you want to know about me?" he asked, again running his fingers through her hair.

She kept her gaze straight ahead. "Actually, you don't have to tell me anything. All I meant was—"

He interrupted. "I love to fly. It's been my passion since I was a boy. I learned when I was in college. They had a flying school just a few miles from campus. Mom thought I was taking a class in aviation history." He grinned. "I was trying to make aviation history. And in a way I did.

"It was my ability to fly a lightweight that got me into trouble in the marines. The idea of being able to take a plane up in foreign airspace was too appealing for me to really look into why Lila wanted me to fly to that village. That and the way she could bat those baby blues of hers." He paused to turn Jana's face so she was looking at him, then he smiled. "Yours aren't blue, but they were just as effective yesterday when you were batting them at me."

Jana lowered her lashes, embarrassed by the truth of what she'd done. "I shouldn't have."

"But you did. Another pretty face that suckered me in. I bet you've broken a lot of hearts."

She shook her head, surprised by the idea. "Actually, I've dated very few men."

"As pretty as you are—intelligent—I find that hard to believe unless it was by choice."

She shrugged. "I guess it was. It's just that I don't want to make a mistake and marry the wrong type of person."

"And what is the wrong type of person?"

Jana knew the answer to that. "Someone in a dangerous occupation, someone who lives on the edge of the law—someone like my father, who might die in my lap, blood running out on the front lawn." She looked at Trevor. "I could never marry someone like you."

"Well, that's a relief off my mind."

And off hers. After the crazy thoughts she'd had the night before, she'd needed to say it, to hear the words aloud. "I'm sure you have lots of women falling all over you, but you're just not my type."

"Well, you're not my type, either."

He said it so adamantly, it bothered her. "And what is your type?"

"Someone who's not out to use me, who will stand by me, through thick and thin." He snorted. "Of course I don't think the female species comes in that model. At least, I've given up trying to find one. I should have listened to my father a long time ago. They used to call him crazy, but believe me, he was as smart as they come. He always said, 'The only thing you can depend on a woman to do is spend your money.' "

"I don't spend much money."

"Honey, you've probably already cost me my plane and my business."

She'd also almost cost him his life. "I'm sorry."

"Yeah, I'll remember that."

"I'd planned on paying you well for this trip."

"But you didn't plan quite far enough ahead, did you? Or tell the truth."

"Sometimes you can't tell the truth." She had learned that as a child. "Sometimes you have to lie to survive."

"Like—" He smiled and fluttered his lashes. " 'I have to take pictures of possible filming sites'?"

"If you'd taken your eyes off my chest, maybe you would have seen how nervous I was about telling you that."

He looked down at her chest, and Jana wished she hadn't said anything. The way she was dressed now made her attire of the day before seem almost modest. Instead of a V to the valley between her breasts, the opening in her blouse reached to the knot below her breasts, and the only part of her breasts that were covered was the flesh near her sides and her nipples, which seemed determined to press against the silk and call attention to themselves.

"And are you nervous now?" he asked, glancing up at her face.

The look in his eyes and his smile said she should be. She swallowed hard. "Yes."

"Afraid?"

That idea surprised her. "Why should I be afraid?"

"No reason at all." He grinned. "I'm not going to do anything you don't want me to do."

She knew that was reason enough to be afraid, especially when he touched the side of her face, grazing a fingertip over her cheek, and she immediately wanted him to kiss her. "Trevor?"

"I think we've had an argument," he said softly. "Want to kiss and make up?"

She did want to, and that scared her. "What we're doing . . . it—it has nothing to do with love."

"Nothing at all," he agreed.

"It's just—"

"Sex." He brushed his lips over hers. "Hormones." Teasingly, he caressed her cheek with the tip of his tongue as he covered one of her breasts with his hand. "Lust."

TEN

Lust, Jana silently repeated as Trevor played his lips over hers. The word said it all. Lust was an intense, unbridled sexual desire. An urge.

What she was feeling had absolutely nothing to do with love. It was hormones—biological chemistry—that had her heart racing. All the while he was kissing her, she kept telling herself she'd be a fool to think it was anything more than lust, on her part as well as his. Trevor was a good-looking man, in excellent physical condition, virile and sexy. She was simply responding as any healthy twenty-eight-year-old female might respond. And why not? They were alone, he had no clothes on, and he wanted her. A simple glance had told her that.

She liked the way he kissed her, his lips investigating all angles of her mouth. She touched his shoulders, running her hands over hard, sinewy muscles. He had always had the strength to overpower her; it had only been a matter of time. But he wasn't using force now. From the very beginning, his gentleness had been her undoing. Force she could have resisted. Concern and tenderness were another matter.

She let her fingers stray to his chest and played a palm across the thick mat of hairs that covered his skin. She felt the thudding of his heart, the rapid beat echoing the rhythm of her own. He was no passive participant. What was exciting her was exciting him.

Inside, she was growing warm and fluid, and she knew the dampness of her panties wasn't entirely due to rain. When he touched her leg, excitement shivered through her, and she held her breath, waiting for him to move his fingers higher. Sparks of pleasure radiated from his hand as he traced a path of seduction over the crotch of her panties. She automatically arched toward his touch, knowing even if she'd wanted to deny her desire, her body was telling him otherwise. He was the wiser for leaving off his clothes. She lifted her hips, letting him ease her out of her panties.

The knot holding her blouse together was released as easily, and the blouse was once more tossed aside. Again, the floor of the cave became their bed, Trevor gently stretching her out before arching his body over her.

"I should hate you," he said, his tone anything but spiteful. "Instead, all I want to do is kiss you . . . touch you. Make love to you."

"Then do it," she said, reaching up to wrap her arms around his neck and draw him closer. "Make love to me, Trevor, until we forget everything and everyone. Until the end of time."

"Until the end of time," he repeated softly.

His kisses traveled from her lips to her cheeks, then he pushed back her hair and explored her ear, wetting it with the tip of his tongue. His warm breath sent shivers through her, and she clutched his sides, writhing beneath him. He traveled on, nibbling his way down her neck, each kiss bringing his head lower until his mouth reached her breasts. There his tongue laved the hard nubs of her nipples, and she shivered more. He sucked and he nibbled, and left her wet and wanting.

She felt his fingers roam lower, distracting her mind and keeping her nerves on edge. For a moment, he played his fingertips over the triangle of hair between her legs, then he moved his hand down, sliding a finger over her most sensitive spot. The contact was light—tantalizing and erotic—and she sucked in her breath, then moaned out her pleasure.

"Do you want me?" he asked, bringing his lips back close to her ear.

"Oh yes." More than she'd thought she'd ever want a man.

"Spread your legs a little," he whispered.

She spread her legs, the rough ground beneath her rubbing against her skin. In contrast, Trevor's kisses were tender. "Yes," he murmured, and touched her, teasing and taunting her with his finger.

Deeper and deeper he explored, driving her wild. She wanted more than what he was giving, wanted him to be a part of her. It wasn't simply a physical need or lust. It defied all reason. One and one did not equal two. With them, she wanted two to be one, united and bonded in body and soul.

Together they would soar, be as strong as the wind and as gentle as a breeze. Together they would forget the differences that held them apart. "Please," she whispered, her need unbearable.

To deny her was impossible and not something Trevor wanted to do. He entered her knowing he was asking for a lifetime of pain. The sweet warmth that encompassed him would haunt his dreams forever, and he would never forget how she looked up at him and smiled as he penetrated her body, before grabbing his shoulders and pulling him down for a kiss.

He could curse her and berate her for the trouble she was causing, but he knew she was worth the price. A man could go a lifetime without experiencing the ecstasy of the perfect lover. He hadn't even known what he was missing, hadn't realized how empty and meaningless his life had become, until Jana stepped through his office door. Only now did he know the true meaning of happiness. Savoring her kisses, he buried himself deep inside her.

The fire raging within him took control, building to a volcanic force. He arched above her, looking down and watching her as he rocked his hips. She groaned, tossing beneath him, her eyes half closed and her lips parted. A sheen of perspiration covered her body as well as his, and her breathing was shallow and ragged. He felt her tighten around him and knew she was close. A touch with his fingers, and her eyes snapped open in surprise.

Even before she could speak, her body exploded around him, and her words became a cry of delight. In those beautiful green eyes with their flecks of gold, he saw her pleasure and knew his own. The rhythmic pulsing of her body took hold of him, and he allowed himself to come with her. They soared, the ecstasy of the moment enveloping him. Paradise became a sensation, a state of mind, and a euphoria that filled him.

After he'd reached that peak, he began to float back down. Slowly—so slowly—he returned to reality. His eyes only half open, he watched her as his body relaxed. Her own eyes were closed, and a smile curved her lips. She looked as satisfied as he felt. His desire was sated, if only for the moment. The fire was banked and his energy drained. Exhausted, he eased himself off her and to her side, gathering her into his arms and holding her close.

He wanted to tell her how much making love with her had meant to him, that maybe they hadn't known each other very long, but that what he was feeling for her was special. He wanted to tell her that she belonged to him and that he was never going to let her go. He wanted to tell her so much, but he said nothing. In silence, he kissed her temple.

He felt her breathing even out and her heartbeat slow. She shifted position, opened her eyes, and looked at him. He kissed her lips, but still he said nothing. She was the one who spoke first. "At least I didn't gouge your back that time," she said.

"A little gouging wouldn't hurt me."

Her eyes held questions he knew she wasn't asking. He didn't pry. The emotions bundled inside him were too near the surface, and he didn't want to chance saying the wrong thing and revealing too much.

The air in the cave stirred, and a flutter of wings

announced the return of some of the birds. Jana twisted in his arms, bringing her hips into contact with his. For a moment, she hesitated, staring at him, then she arched her neck to look outside. "Clouds are back," she said. "And the wind."

"And thus ends the calm."

She turned back to him and smiled. "That was the calm? Felt pretty wild to me."

"Complaining?"

"No." Her grin illustrated her satisfaction. "It is one way to while away the time during a hurricane."

"A good way, as far as I'm concerned." He already felt a renewed desire for her. "You know, this storm is probably going to last a few hours."

Jana laughed. "I can see it now. They'll find us some-time after this hurricane has passed. We'll be dead, our bodies entwined. Coroner's report: died from making love too many times. Another casualty of the storm."

"Ah, but what a way to go."

"What a way," she agreed, and kissed him on his shoulder.

They made love again, then talked for a while. The wind became wild and thunderous and the rain returned, once again forming a waterfall in front of the mouth of the cave. The birds all returned, but were disturbed by the movement at the back of the cave. Jana could imagine what they were thinking, if birds thought, especially when Trevor made love to her for a third time that morning.

It was afternoon when she and Trevor ventured near the entrance of the cave, using the spray of water to bathe their bodies and satisfy their thirst. With his arm around her shoulders, they stood and watched as nature displayed its power, the wind churning up the water in the sea below, the sky a turbulent mass of dark clouds. She wondered what was happening outside their sheltered world, how the people she'd met the night before were dealing with the wind and the rain and all that had happened because of her.

Only briefly did she think about her stepbrother. She found it impossible to care if he was alive or dead, perhaps because she was sure he was dead. She didn't want to think about Trevor's plane, and she didn't ask him what he thought might be happening to it. For the moment, she didn't want to remind him that she was the enemy. In all the chaos of the last two months, she'd found one settling element, and that was Trevor. His kisses had unlocked a part of her she'd never known existed, and his touch made her feel like the woman she'd always been afraid to be.

She shivered, and he led her back to where they were sheltered from the wind and the cold. He sat first and pulled her down on his lap, wrapping his arms around her. "I suppose," she said, "you're going to give me that 'two bodies are warmer than one' story again."

He grinned. "Worked the first time, didn't it?"

"You did get me warm," she admitted.

"Got us talking."

"Hmm, is that what you call it?" She nibbled on his earlobe.

"Jana." He laughed and slipped a hand down to her hip. "You are insatiable."

"Just a good little Catholic girl who's discovered sex." She leaned back a little. "I don't suppose you're Catholic."

"Nope. I guess you could say I'm officially nothing."

"I stopped going to mass after my father was killed. I guess I'm officially nothing."

"So should we be married in the 'officially nothing' church?"

The idea of marrying Trevor took her breath away. She stared at him, a strange, very right feeling building in her. It didn't make sense, but she didn't question it. She simply knew it would be right, that he would be there when she needed him, as he had been from the moment they'd met, and he would stick by her side and protect her and love her.

His laugh shattered her thoughts. "As if we would ever get married," he said. "Talk about a ridiculous thought."

She swallowed her disappointment and smiled. "Totally ridiculous."

The storm abated near dusk. Trevor's stomach growled about the same time. "I don't know about you," he said, "but I am hungry."

Jana had passed the point of hunger hours ago, but the thought of food renewed the pangs. "I could even eat that fish head now without blinking an eye."

"I suggest we go see what damage Ned did and if we can find something to eat."

They'd put on their clothes in the late afternoon and now they pulled on their socks and shoes. Jana's were still damp, and when Trevor took a step, she heard his boots squish. Not that she thought it would matter. Where they were headed had just been doused by several inches of rain and wouldn't have had a chance to dry.

She followed Trevor to the mouth of the cave. The birds flew off, squalling their displeasure at having their nesting site invaded by humans. Glancing back into the cave's interior, she wondered how many others had taken shelter in its confines over the centuries, and what acts of intrigue and romance had been played out in the same space she and Trevor had used to make love.

Although she knew they couldn't stay, she was reluctant to leave. Here she'd been safe, had discovered how exciting making love could be, and had shared the stories of her life with Trevor. No longer were they strangers. He knew her body better than any other man, knew about her childhood and her teens, her college days and her struggle to succeed in the world of banking. In turn, she'd learned about his mistakes, about how he'd disappointed his mother and had never truly understood his father. She knew how much he loved flying, and that intensified her feelings of guilt. Considering the fury of the storm, she feared the worst for his plane.

"It's slippery," he said as he started up the path that had led them to the cave.

Cautiously she climbed after him, accepting his hand when he offered to help her and taking her time. The waves crashing against the rocks below would not forgive a misstep, and she wondered how they'd made it down. Fear had goaded her on then. Even now, it gripped her stomach and kept her looking up at the summit. Every step she took, she expected to see Alvarez or one of his men.

When at last they reached level ground, she paused to look back down. If she hadn't known it was there, she never would have guessed the presence of a cave. Trevor had hidden them well.

Standing beside him, she realized Trevor did many things well, from staying calm in a crisis to arousing her in passion. He slid an arm around her shoulders and gave her a gentle hug, taking care not to press against her bruise, and she knew she trusted him. Not that she deserved his trust after all she'd put him through, nor did she understand why he'd protected her. She only knew, leaning against his side and looking over the devastation in front of them, she felt at one with him.

Daylight was rapidly fading, and the woods were enshrouded in deep shadows. The insects and frogs that had been silenced by the storm were gathering forces and starting their night songs. The lone call of a bird lent an eerie note to the ensemble, while the shadowy silhouette of the pine that had fallen earlier, its roots torn from the ground and its limbs broken and crushed, added to the haunting atmosphere.

Jana stared at the tree, sensing an analogy. She might be on her feet, but she'd been torn from all she knew. Life as she'd known it was over.

"Come on," Trevor urged, and led her around the

downed tree. "We need to get going while we still have some light."

They went as quickly as they could back toward the inhabited end of the island. The wind had died down and mosquitoes discovered them before they'd gone halfway. Trevor heard Jana slapping at them and cursing with every step she took. He clenched his teeth when they attacked him, and wished he'd had the foresight to bring repellent along.

The hurricane's damage was everywhere. All around them were washouts, downed trees, broken branches, and shattered limbs. Water ran in rivulets along any depression, and Trevor knew the marshes would be impassable and was glad he hadn't chosen to go back into them. The water-soaked ground sucked at his boots, threatening to mire him or send him toppling. He held onto Jana's hand, carefully guiding her around the obstacles and back to humanity.

He knew they couldn't have stayed in the cave, but he was nervous at leaving its safety. Ahead was the unknown, the danger they'd fled possibly even greater than before. Reason told him to take her to the most remote area of the island, that there, like Robinson Crusoe, they could live off the land until he was sure all was safe. But hiding out wouldn't resolve her dilemma. He had to find a way to get her off the island and prove her innocence.

It was dark by the time they reached the edge of the woods and the village. The clouds were breaking, and glimpses of moonlight illuminated the panorama in front of them. Hurricane Ned had not been kind to Cayton. Roofs had been torn from housetops, walls toppled, and trees downed. Water covered streets and yards, the shallow lake created by both the rain and oversized waves. Those houses nearest the beach had fared the worst. Some had been completely demolished; others were tilted at an angle, their foundations all but washed away. Down by the dock, Groaners Bar remained standing, along with Cora's trading post, but the bait shop was gone, only the carved fishing pole that had stood in front of the shop still reaching to the sky.

Fishing boats sat beached on land or straddled what was left of the wooden dock. Curious, Trevor angled over so he could see the house his father had lived in for so many years. The sight was depressing. Between the damage the waves had inflicted and a fallen tree, little remained of the front of the house, and the back half was leaning at a precarious angle. It would no longer be housing anyone: crazy painter or ruthless robbers.

He worked his way back toward the airstrip, knowing he wouldn't like what he found. At first he didn't see any planes, then he realized the shadowy pile by the storage shed was the entangled wreckage of two planes. Wrapped together, Alvarez's Piper Warrior was almost on end and leaning on the Navajo. Trevor knew neither of the aircraft would be airborne in the near future, if ever. Escape by plane was no longer an option, and considering the condition of the fishing boats, escape by that means didn't look much more promising.

The islanders were in the streets, surveying the damage to their homes and consoling one another. Trevor glanced from group to group, looking for men with lighter skins. The only light-skinned person he saw was female. "Tia," he murmured, and led Jana in that direction.

He worked his way closer to Tia, always keeping an eye out for Alvarez and his men or Jana's stepbrother and his men. He was not about to lose what he had found. If Jana walked away from him, it would be on her terms.

He stayed in the shadows when he called to Tia. At first she looked at Lynden, then behind her. Trevor repeated her name and knew the moment she saw him. Quickly she came over.

Wrapping her arms around him, she gave him a hug. "Hey, man, you scared us. When we heard those gun shots, we thought you were goners."

"It wasn't exactly a fun situation. How about you and the others? Anyone hurt?"

"No. We all okay. No one from the island hurt. Steve and one of the others, though, they dead. Washed away with the storm." Tia made a flowing motion with her hand toward the beach.

"My stepbrother?" Jana asked, keeping her voice low.

Tia stepped back from Trevor and looked at Jana. Although visibility was limited, he was sure Tia could see the whisker burns on Jana's face and how her lips were swollen from so many kisses. Judging by his half sister's smile, she knew they'd been doing more than simply surviving a hurricane.

"He not dead," Tia said, then looked at Trevor. "Your father's house not good. You see?"

"I saw. How much damage to yours?"

"Not bad. Funny. Just last week I complain to

Lynden because we so far from beach. Now, I'm happy."
Tia touched Jana's wrinkled blouse. "You stay dry?"

"Trevor took me to a cave. We stayed pretty dry."

Tia grinned at Trevor. "How friendly."

"Very friendly," he agreed, certain Tia understood.
"But no food and we're starved."

"Always hungry." She laughed. "Okay, man, I have
food. Candy bars, too, though some missing from before." She grinned. "You have any idea why?"

"No idea at all."

Her grin widened. "Come. You will eat, and we will
talk. We need to talk."

Tia went back to Lynden and spoke to him. He
glanced their way, then came over. "Hey man, good to
see you," he said, shaking Trevor's hand. "Once again,
the Fox survives."

"I told you he would," Tia said proudly. "I'm taking
them back to the house. Give them some food. Show
them our surprise."

"Surprise?" Trevor asked.

"You see." Again, she grinned, her teeth flashing
white in the darkness. "You see."

Trevor followed her, keeping Jana by his side. He had
no idea what Tia's surprise might be. He'd had enough
surprises in the last two days. He was beginning to think
he wanted what Jana had said she wanted: a quiet, un-
eventful life. Of course, what she said she wanted and
what she created around her were two very different
things.

Tia and Lynden's home looked like a houseboat in a
vast lake. The three of them sloshed through water up to

their knees, and the porch creaked as they climbed the steps, but when Tia opened the door, it was evident the house was in fairly good shape. Some rain had blown through the louvered windows, and the floor and woven palm mats were wet in places, but there was no mud or sand.

Tia didn't bother to turn on a lamp, but headed straight for the second bedroom. Trevor followed. A beaded curtain was all that separated the room from the rest of the house. Tia pushed it aside and stepped into the room. Trevor heard a muffled sound, but it wasn't until Tia lit a candle that he understood. The glow of the flickering light barely illuminated the small room, turning everything shadowy. He looked toward the bed and smiled.

ELEVEN

A spark of hope flared in Jana. Lying on the bed, his hands and feet tied to the wrought-iron frame and a wide piece of duct tape across his mouth, was her stepbrother. He had a bruise on his chin, probably where he'd hit the porch when Trevor tackled him the night before, but otherwise he looked fine. Upset, but fine.

"Jeff." She wasn't sure if she wanted to hug him for being alive or slug him for all he'd put her through.

He grunted and glared at her, obviously not sharing any thoughts of hugs. Trevor asked Tia the logical question. "How'd he end up here?"

"We trap him." Tia smiled proudly and walked over to the bed, placing a hand on the bed frame as if showing off a wild animal she had captured. "He comes out of the woods, and Turk, he catches him. He is the one you want. Right, man?"

"Exactly right," Trevor said.

Jeff made a sound that resembled a growl, and Jana stepped closer to the end of the bed. "Why?" she asked.

Tia reached down and ripped the tape from Jeff's mouth. Jana flinched at the sound and Jeff swore, his glare switching to Tia. "She asked a question, man," Tia said, scowling right back at Jeff. Then she looked at Jana and Trevor. "He's not being cooperative. Doesn't eat. Complains."

"You call that food?" Jeff snarled. "It's more like eating fire."

"No hair off my back if you starve, man," Tia said.

Jeff switched his attention to Jana. "You've got to get me out of here."

"Gladly," she agreed. "Out of here and straight to the police. Why did you do it, Jeff? I thought they'd kidnapped you, thought you were as much a victim as I was."

He snorted. "Why do you think I did it? For the money, of course. You said yourself, that night at the dinner table, that the amount in that one account was mind boggling." He smiled, his self-satisfaction blatant. "Well now, instead of boggling Mr. Alvarez's mind, that money is in accounts that can boggle my mind."

"Whatever good that's going to do you." She certainly couldn't think of any way he'd ever be able to enjoy the money. "Alvarez and his men aren't playing games. They came here to kill you."

The glare returned to Jeff's eyes, mingled with shards of hatred. "Alvarez wouldn't have had the slightest idea where to find me if you hadn't led him here."

"Oh yeah? And what makes you think that if I could find you, Alvarez couldn't?"

She knew he had no answer for that, and she was sure she was right. Without Uncle Nicky, she wouldn't have tracked her stepbrother to Conch Island. But if Nicholas Scarlotti could find Jeff, others could too. "You sure didn't plan this out very well."

"Must be a family trait," she heard Trevor say under his breath. She ignored him.

"Who had the time to plan?" Jeff answered. "You said Alvarez would be transferring the money the end of the week."

"One comment during dinner and you turn into a thief?" She found that hard to believe.

"Opportunity knocked and I answered." He chuckled at his own joke, then turned serious. "It wasn't the first time I've transferred money from one account to another. Being a hacker does have its advantages. All I need is a means of access. After that, it's easy."

"You are a thief." The realization sickened her.

"And a damned good one."

"Oh great. Brag about it. Do you realize the trouble you've caused? I hijacked this man's plane to come rescue you." She pointed at Trevor. "Now it's a pile of scrap metal."

"Tish, tish." Jeff grinned.

"Why you—!"

Jana lunged forward, and Trevor decided it was time to step in. Quickly, he pulled her back. "Don't waste your energy, honey."

"Honey?" Jeff repeated mockingly. "What happened to that wimp you were going out with in Michigan?"

"Oh, you took care of that romance," Jana said bitterly. "In fact, you've messed up my life completely."

"But leave it to you to find a half-wit to come to your rescue."

Trevor felt Jana tense. "He is not a half-wit."

"Oh sure." Jeff's smile was as cruel as it was mocking. "Mr. Intelligence here, who lets a female half his size hijack his plane. You'll make a wonderful couple."

This time when Jana tried to lunge at Jeff, Trevor was tempted to let her. Instead he interceded. "Don't let him get to you."

She glanced up at him. "He has no right to call you names."

"He's just trying to upset you."

She huffed, then shook her head and again looked at Jeff. "Go ahead and make fun of Trevor, and make light of what happened to his plane, but let me tell you, if Alvarez survived that hurricane, you're going to wish that plane was in operating condition. Alvarez and his men have already killed two or three of your men."

"So I've been told." Jeff's attitude remained smug. "But who needs a plane? I've got a boat."

"Boats one big mess," Tia said, the announcement given with a shake of her head. "Everything big mess." She looked at Jana. "I think all you people coming to island anger spirits."

"It wasn't her," Trevor said, afraid of what might happen if the islanders did start believing that Jana was the cause of the hurricane and their problems. He nodded toward Jeff. "He's the one who touched something he shouldn't have. Jana came to make him put it back."

Tia shook a finger at Jeff. "You should have heeded warning of *obeah*."

"Obey?" Jeff laughed at her.

Trevor could see that Jana didn't understand, either, and explained. "*Obeah* are bottles filled with liquid spells. It's a form of voodoo practiced on some of the islands. The *obeah* is hung from a tree near the crops, or here they hang them on their boats. It's a warning to others to keep their hands off."

"I guess we needed one in the bank," Jana said.

"Should always have one," Tia said, her gaze darting between the two of them. "So now that you've seen our big surprise, you ready to eat?"

"Sounds good to me," Trevor answered. Being shot at, surviving a hurricane, and making love through the night and day had a way of making him hungry. And considering how Jana was reacting to her stepbrother's digs, it was time to get her out of the room. "Come on, let's eat and deal with him later."

She hesitated, then she released a deep breath and nodded. "You're right. I'm so tired and hungry, I can't think straight."

"I fix something simple." Tia started from the room. Immediately, Jeff started yelling, ordering her to come back and untie him. Grinning, Tia returned to Jeff's side. With one quick movement, she placed the tape back across his mouth. Trevor couldn't think of a better way of dealing with the situation.

In the kitchen, Tia lit several candles and a battery

lamp, then went to a cupboard. As she opened it, Jana spoke up. "I want to thank you, Tia . . . for everything you and the others have done."

Tia looked back at her. "Last two days, we have more excitement than we have in a long time."

"In the last two months, I've had more than I wanted." Jana sighed. "I just wish I could get back to Michigan and my life as it was."

Tia lifted her eyebrows. "Why you want to go to Michigan? Cold in Michigan."

Trevor remembered how cold it got in New York and why he had no desire to go back.

"When it gets cold," Jana answered, "you stay inside, where it's warm."

Tia looked at him. "You always say you no like the cold. Get cold here during storm. More cold than I ever remember. The both of you stay warm?"

"We did our best to," he said, smiling as he recalled their efforts.

"Good." Tia turned back to the cupboard and pulled out two cans. "I tell Lynden you be okay. You smart man." She looked at Jana. "Is your stepbrother who is the dimwit, I think."

"I agree," Jana said, and smiled at Trevor.

Trevor wondered, though. How smart was it to fall in love with a woman who only wanted her old life back? The hours they'd spent in the cave seemed like a dream. Then they'd had no future, only the present. Now, with her stepbrother alive, things were different. If they could get Jeff to the authorities, Jana's name could be cleared. She could return to Michigan and her life as it had been.

And what would happen to him?

He knew the answer without being told. It would be the same as what had happened to him before. He would have served his purpose and be forgotten. Maybe Jana hadn't planned this as well as Lila had planned her caper, but the results would be the same. Once this was over, he would be left, just as his plane would be left, a tangled wreckage with no further use.

He turned away from her and headed for the door. "I'm going to go take a look at my plane, see how bad the damage is. I'll be back in a while."

Trevor's abrupt departure surprised Jana. After having him by her side for so many hours, she felt as if a part of her was walking out the door. She longed to go with him, but stood where she was, knowing once he examined his plane, he would hate her. For a brief space of time he'd forgotten she'd forced him to fly her here, and that she'd put him in a situation he couldn't avoid. For a while, they'd simply been a man and a woman getting to know each other. Two people falling in love. Now reality surrounded them.

"Something disturbs him," Tia said, and Jana turned to face her again.

"It's his plane." She shook her head. "I never should have made him fly me here."

"Trevor does what he wants. He is like his father. Sometimes what he does seems crazy, but it's not."

"Was Trevor's father crazy?"

Tia shrugged, then smiled. "Crazy like a fox. He gets what he wants. Lives way he wants. That crazy?"

"I don't think so."

"I know your stepbrother wrong. Trevor, he is very smart. When I little, he reads to me about the stars and the planets and we talk about people and the future of the world. Lynden and Wally, they always tease Trevor, say he's smart like a fox."

"He said you two think you have the same father."

Tia laughed and held out her arm. "What you think? That Gaddy and my mother produce skin this color? I think they like keeping a secret that everyone knows. I think it a secret that is not a secret."

Jana understood those kinds of secrets. For years she and her mother had thought they were keeping their identities secret. But it was no secret, not to the Family, at least. And their secret was easily discovered by the FBI once they began checking into her background. "Trevor thinks the world of you."

"I think maybe his world now involves you. How you feel about that?"

"I think it's not going to matter how I feel. Even if we get off this island and I get this robbery mess straightened out, he's going to be so mad at me, he'll probably want to hang me from the nearest tree."

"Trevor gets mad quickly, but then he forgives."

Jana thought of Trevor's plane, all twisted and scrunched against the shed, the second plane on top of it. "I think it would take a saint to forgive me for what I've done."

Tia arched her eyebrows, her smile momentarily gone. "If you are that bad, I do not understand why he looks at you like he does."

"Wait until he comes back from his plane. See how

he looks at me then." Jana nodded toward the cans Tia had set on the counter. "Anything I can do to help with the cooking?"

Tia continued to study her, her expression serious, then the smile returned. "I think, lady, the Fox knows exactly what he is doing. You open cans, and we will fix a very good meal."

The soup was ready by the time Trevor returned. With him were Lynden, Gaddy, and Olive. Perhaps it was simply because he was hungry that he went straight to the table and sat down without saying a word. Jana could see that Tia noticed Trevor's silence. The younger woman's glance darted from Trevor to Jana, then she turned back to the stove.

Jana helped serve the soup. Trevor mumbled a thank you when she set his bowl in front of him. That was all. He didn't look at her. Didn't touch her.

The only chairs empty by the time she and Tia had everyone served were next to Trevor and Lynden. Feeling Tia's place was next to her husband, Jana sat next to Trevor. He reached for a bottle of beer.

Olive, Lynden, and Gaddy gave their assessment of the damage to the village and the boats. Then Gaddy asked the question Jana had been dreading. "What you find, man, with da planes?"

Jana felt Trevor's quick, cool glance. "I don't think either can be salvaged."

She winced at his words, though they didn't surprise her. She'd seen the planes earlier. She'd even known he would act this way, though it didn't make it any easier. Only a few inches separated their chairs, but a block of ice was wedged between them. All because she'd made a total mess of everything.

"Any sign of Alvarez?" she finally asked.

Lynden and Gaddy shook their heads. "Last time we see him, he was after you. His men, they shoot those two that wash away, then go into the woods. When we hear more shots, we think you both dead. Later, we find the one you say is your stepbrother. He says he doesn't know what happens to you, that you not dead, so we decide to tie him up and wait until storm over to see what happens."

"We need to get him to the police as soon as possible," Trevor said. "Need to get him out of this house and off this island. With Alvarez still around, he's trouble."

Jana understood what he was saying. She'd not only messed up his life, she was messing up everyone's life. Selfishly, she'd thought of her welfare, not of anyone else's.

She said nothing.

Gaddy spoke between spoonfuls of soup. "If Charlie's radio still works, we can call out in da morning. Hard saying, I think, when anyone comes here. Dis storm a bad one."

"I said it would be." Olive looked at each of them, waiting for agreement.

Trevor gave it to her. "And you were right."

"Storm like this one comes every thirty, forty years. We have the big one in '65. It does lots of damage. When your father comes here, I tell him not take house so close to water. But he doesn't listen. You see the house?"

"I saw it," Trevor said. "And I remember your telling him someday a storm would blow that house away."

"I know some things not last," Olive said. "No matter how good they look at moment. I right about that Italian. Everyone think he help us and he nearly burn down the village." She looked at Trevor. "I right about your father. He now gone." Her gaze switched to Gaddy, and she smiled. "I right about my Gaddy. He still here."

"You smart lady," Gaddy said, beaming.

Jana wished the same could be said about her. It seemed as if she'd made one stupid mistake after another. She never should have mentioned Alvarez or his money to anyone. She shouldn't have listened to Uncle Nicky when he told her Trevor was the one she should hire to fly her here, that he deserved anything that happened to him. Even leaving her handbag on the plane had been stupid. In it, she'd had the money she'd planned on paying Trevor. The last time she'd seen her handbag, one of the robbers had had it. Where it was now, was anyone's guess. Either floating out to sea or . . .

She looked over at Lynden and Gaddy. "Has anyone been in that house since my stepbrother and the others came out to watch our diversion?"

"I don't think so," Gaddy answered. "First was da shooting, den da running. After that comes da rain and da wind. No time for anyone to go into da house."

"The way that house looks," Trevor said, "no one better go into it."

Maybe, Jana thought, but if there was a chance her

handbag and her money were still in the house, it might be worth the risk. Her savings wouldn't pay for the damage to Trevor's plane, but it would help.

Gaddy and Olive left after they'd eaten. Tia got up to clear the table, and Jana helped. Trevor watched her, all the while trying to concentrate on Lynden's description of the storm when it hit. "I tell you, man, those waves were like a wall of water. They kept coming up higher and higher." He held his hand about eighteen inches high. "Chickens and goats, they go floating by." He laughed and pointed at Jana. "Her stepbrother, he says if we let him loose, he help save animals. Me, I know what he do if we let him loose." Lynden waved toward the bedrooms. "Bye-bye."

Jana walked back to the table. "Thank you for catching him and keeping him here."

"No problem." Lynden looked over at Trevor. "Only problem is, where you two gonna sleep tonight? You want we should take her stepbrother off the bed?"

"No," Trevor said. "Leave him there. You've got him tied securely." He'd checked. "The living room floor will be fine for me." Especially since he didn't plan on getting much sleep, not with Alvarez's whereabouts unknown. He looked Jana's way. "What about you?"

Her gaze met his, and he wondered at the sadness he saw in her eyes. Then she looked away. "It doesn't matter. I can sleep anywhere."

Trevor made up his mind. "She'll share the floor with me."

◆————————◆

Jana appreciated the simplicity of Tia and Lynden's house. Although rain had blown in the windows, wetting the rug, Lynden and Trevor simply rolled it up and took it out on the porch to dry. A rubbing of rags over the floor boards removed most of the excess moisture from the wood, then Tia came out with a sleeping bag. "A woman left it," she said as she spread the bag on the floor. "Plane brings her to Conch. She says she's going to live on the beach and write a book about island. Two days later, she asks Charlie to call for plane to come get her. Leaves lots of things when she goes. You want something to sleep in? She leaves nightgown I never use."

Jana glanced down at her wrinkled and soiled blouse and slacks. "I look pretty bad, don't I?"

"You pretty woman. You look good in this nightgown. You ever see a book about woman living two days on an island?"

"No." Though Jana felt she could write one herself.

"I think she a little crazy."

Jana watched Trevor walk back into the room, and wondered if the island turned everyone crazy. She had to be out of her mind. She was asking for heartache, but she couldn't wait to be alone with him.

Trevor sat in the wicker chair and waited for Jana to come out of the bathroom. Through the walls, he could hear the murmurings of Tia and Lynden as they prepared for bed. He'd checked on Jeff earlier, finding him asleep.

Outside, the street still looked like a lake. People had gone inside to dry off and sleep. All was peaceful, and he was as tense as a spring.

The bathroom door opened, and he saw the glow of Jana's candle. Her steps were hesitant, and he waited, knowing he was holding his breath. The moment she came into view, she paused, her gaze locking with his.

She was wearing a short sleeved pale pink cotton gown that was scooped at the neckline and barely came to her knees. It was loose fitting and simple in its design, its pattern indiscernible at a distance. In his opinion, it covered much too much of her.

"It felt good to wash," she said, remaining where she was. "Where do they get their water?"

"From rain. They collect it in a gravity tank." He stood and took a step forward. "Where'd you get the nightgown?"

"Tia gave it to me." Jana glanced down, running her hand along her side and pressing the fabric against her skin.

The gesture gave him a good view of the outline of her breasts. Her nipples were hard and dimpled the cotton. He swallowed, feeling a physical response within his body. "Do you have anything on under that?"

She kept her gaze lowered. "No."

The response within his body became more defined. "That could be very tempting to a man marooned on a deserted island."

She looked up, smiling slightly. "This isn't exactly a deserted island."

"Not exactly."

He saw her take in a deep breath and expel it. "After seeing your plane, you probably hate me, and I—"

"Hatred is not what I'm feeling."

"What I mean is, you have every right to hate me, and—"

"Come here."

She stared at him, then took a step in his direction. He met her halfway, taking the candle from her hand and blowing it out before dropping it to the floor. He gathered her into his arms and heard her sigh. "I'm so sorry," she whispered.

He kissed her into silence. Olive was right. Some things didn't last. When Jana was gone and out of his life, he would think about his plane and about hating her, but for now, he only wanted to love her. Bunching up the cotton of her nightgown, he slipped his hands underneath. He ran his fingers up the backs of her legs, cupping her bottom and drawing her hips against his. Her softness fit his hardness, and he knew with a touch that she was ready for him. His zipper went down, then his trousers. Holding her close, he rubbed against her, teasing himself as he stimulated her.

"Oh yes," she murmured against his lips.

"Do you want me?" he asked, needing the words.

Her yes was covered by another voice. "Hey, man, Tia thought you might like . . ."

Lynden's voice trailed off, and Trevor looked over Jana's shoulder. Lynden grinned a silly grin, dropped a blanket over a chair, and backed out of the room.

TWELVE

It was daylight when Jana woke. The blanket Lynden had left was scrunched down around her hips and the space next to her on the spread-out sleeping bag was empty; nevertheless, she knew Trevor was nearby. Rolling to her side, she saw him.

He'd pulled the wicker chair closer to the window and was looking out. For a moment, she watched him, memorizing his features. In the last two days, she'd learned so much about him. He'd called himself a sucker, and in the beginning, she'd played him for one. Now she knew his weakness was that he cared about people. He was a nice guy, and she'd put him into a situation that was not only endangering his life, but also ruining his livelihood. If Nicholas Scarlotti had sent her to Trevor so she would be protected, he'd served her well, but Jana wouldn't thank him. How could she? In Trevor, she'd found a man she could love, but once they got off this island, he would be lost to her forever.

If they ever got off the island.

A mosquito buzzed her head, and she swatted at it. Trevor looked her way, then smiled. "Morning, sunshine."

"Morning, yourself." She rose and walked over to him, stretching cramped muscles as she did. She wasn't used to this much lovemaking. Heck, she wasn't used to any of this.

Stopping beside him, she leaned over to look out the window. "What are you watching?"

"Nothing." He pulled her down on his lap, nuzzling her neck as he wrapped his arms around her waist, one hand fondling a breast.

His beard had two days of growth and tickled her skin. She squealed and giggled, then leaned into him, sighing with contentment. "Ah, this is the life. A little armed conflict mixed with a hurricane blended in with hours of lovemaking."

"I'm game," he whispered.

She laughed. "You're insatiable."

"What are you two laughing at?" Tia asked, stepping into the living room.

Jana felt her cheeks flame as Trevor dropped his hand from her breast. He answered Tia. "Inside joke."

Scooting off Trevor's lap, Jana straightened her nightgown and glanced at the bedding on the floor. "Thanks for the blanket."

Tia grinned. "No problem. Sometimes when people not joking, they get cold at night." She looked at Trevor. "I was wondering if you could help Lynden with our friend in the bedroom. He needs go bathroom and be fed."

"Sure." Trevor looked out the window again, checking in both directions, then stood. He paused as he passed Tia. "Keep an eye out for our South American friends, okay?"

"Okay, man. Is good idea." Tia held out a hand to Jana. "You, come with me. We find you some clothes. Make you an islander."

Trevor looked up from the egg he was feeding Jeff as Jana stepped into the room. She looked different wearing a colorful cotton blouse and wraparound skirt. Her hair was pulled back with a piece of red cloth, and she wore no shoes. If her skin had been darker and her eyes brown instead of green, she might have passed as one of the locals. In his opinion, she was simply beautiful.

"About time you showed up," Jeff snarled as she neared the bed. "Get me out of here."

"As soon as we can, we will." As she stopped beside Trevor's chair, he caught the scent of something familiar and sniffed. She smiled and shrugged. "Tia said it's a mosquito repellant. I thought people used it to keep their skin soft. I know my skin feels oily now."

He ran a fingertip over her bare arm, smoothing the fine hairs that covered her skin and feeling a slippery glaze. "Stay out of the sun. You can get a nasty burn with that stuff on."

Jeff snorted. "Isn't that sweet. He's worried about

you. No question about what he's getting out of this deal."

Trevor refused to dignify the comment with more than a look, but he could feel Jana bristle beside him. "You want to know what he's getting?" she said. "He's getting a smashed up plane and in trouble with the FAA. And it's all because of you and me."

"Oh, I think he's getting something more than that." Jeff looked at Trevor. "You should thank me. Normally she'd never look at someone like you. My little sister here likes her men to be ambitious and sophisticated. On their way up the corporate ladder."

"I am not your little sister," Jana snapped. "And those were Phil's words, not mine."

"If you say so, *stepsister*," Jeff said. "But you made it clear someone like me wasn't in the ball game. Only time you agreed to go out with me was when you thought you'd get something from me." He sneered. " 'Oh yes, if you'll show me how to work that program, I'll take you to dinner,' " he said in a falsetto voice, then dropped it back to normal when he spoke to Trevor. "You want to make a deal?"

"What kind of a deal?"

"A trade." Jeff jerked on the ropes holding him tied to the bed, and the metal frame creaked and jiggled. "I want out of here. You just lost a plane and need a new one. You get me off this island to someplace safe, and I'll see to it that you not only have enough money to buy a new plane, you can buy a fleet of planes."

"Oh great!" Jana said before Trevor could respond. "Now you're trying bribery. Well, you can forget it.

Trevor doesn't take bribes. And you can forget that money. It's probably been washed out to sea. Your little hideaway is barely standing."

"Do you really think I had all that money in that house?" Jeff shook his head, the bed again creaking. "Maybe the book with the list of banks and account numbers has been lost, but I don't need that. I know everywhere we transferred that money. It's all in my head."

He looked so smug, Trevor wanted to jam the spoonful of egg he held right down Jeff's throat. Instead, he kept him talking. "I can't understand why you came to Conch Island in the first place."

"To let things cool down. It was definitely getting too hot around Detroit. My man, Stevarino, used to say Conch Island was so backward, it was like living in the past. That no one ever came here—no one but that crazy artist who used to live in the house we took over. And since he was dead, he wasn't going to object to our using it."

Jeff looked at Jana. "We didn't leave Michigan right away. I saw the papers. Saw how you were a hero one day, then a suspect the next. What a surprise to discover my sweet little stepsister was the daughter of a Mafia hit man." He grinned. "Who would have guessed? Had I known, I might have let you in on this deal."

"I have never done anything illegal in my life." She paused, and Trevor saw a flash of guilt in her eyes and knew she was thinking of the hijacking. Then she looked back at her stepbrother. "That is, I hadn't until you turned me into this creature who goes around carrying a concealed weapon and shooting at people."

"You always acted so prim and proper, you made me sick." From his position on the bed, Jeff scanned her figure. "You should thank me. At least you now look like a real woman."

Jana looked down at the colorful blouse and sarong skirt Tia had given her to wear. The outfit was certainly different from the power suits hanging in her closet back in Michigan. "I suppose you think I should be flattered by that."

"A little flattery never hurt, they say."

"I don't think you're taking this seriously, Jeff. This is not a game. You should not have touched the money in Alvarez's account. The man is out to get you."

Jeff shook his head. "He won't touch me. Not as long as I know where his money is." He smiled, his expression self-satisfied. "When did he find out it was gone?"

It was a game to Jeff, and that irked her. But then, he hadn't been cornered by Alvarez, hadn't seen the cold hatred in the man's eyes or heard his steely threats delivered in that soft Hispanic accent. Alvarez had said her life depended on her getting his money back. She'd believed him. This wasn't a joke for her. "You're a fool, Jeff. A complete fool."

His smile disappeared, replaced by anger. "You're the fool. Considering how little time I had to plan all this, I think I pulled off a pretty snazzy caper. You never hesitated to type your password in right in front of me. And when I pulled that plug, you even did it again. I mean, how dumb can you get?" He didn't wait for her answer.

"How long did it take them to fix that problem in the data banks?"

"How did you know about that?" As far as she knew, it hadn't been mentioned in the papers.

His grin returned. "Who do you think put that glitch there?"

"I should have known." But he was right, she had been too dumb to realize he could figure out her password simply by watching her type it in. Too dumb to accept that he was behind everything that happened that day. "Alvarez was suspicious right from the beginning," she said, remembering the South American's fury when he walked into the bank. "He came storming in less than twenty minutes after the robbery. How he'd heard about it, I don't know. He started yelling that he wanted his money transferred to Swiss accounts right then. And when we couldn't get any of the computers to work, he started ranting that we were imbeciles and his money was gone."

Jeff seemed pleased with what she'd said. "You know why you couldn't get any of the computers to work? Because I was transferring the money then. Didn't take me long. The moment I was in the van and we took off, I was making a phone connection with the bank's system and typing in your password. In ten minutes, the transfers were being made. What the other four got in cash was piddling compared with what I took out of that bank electronically."

"And the ransom note to your dad?"

"Just a diversion. Something to muddy the waters while we made arrangements to get out of the country."

He looked at Trevor. "So we're back to my question. What's it going to take for you to get me off this island? And I don't mean to the police."

Jana looked down at the top of Trevor's head, expecting to hear him laugh at Jeff's suggestion. Instead, Trevor leaned back in his chair and stared up at the ceiling. "I don't know. What I saw last night of the fishing boats wasn't good. They're going to need repairs before they're safe in the water. Which leaves a guy who has a shortwave radio, which may or may not be working."

"Forget the radio," Jeff said. "A radio won't help. There's gotta be one boat around here that will float." He laughed. "Hell, this island has trees. Build a raft."

Again, instead of scoffing at the idea, Trevor nodded. "Once these waters calm down a little," he said, "we might be able to use the inflatable raft that's on my plane. Cost me enough. Should work."

"Yeah, a rubber raft might do it," Jeff said, looking more relaxed. "So how long before the waters calm down?"

Trevor shrugged. "A few hours. Maybe a day."

"You're going to help him." Jana stared at Trevor, unable to explain the feeling of betrayal cutting through her.

Trevor looked up at her. "What do you think?"

"I think you're disgusting." She turned on her heel and walked out of the room. Behind her, she heard Jeff snicker.

The water had gone down during the night, so only puddles of it covered the ground here and there. Lynden had left for the docks earlier, and Jana found Tia outside, inspecting the damage to her yard. Jana was so angry, she wanted to do some damage herself, primarily to one double-crossing pilot who she'd thought was noble and honorable and on her side. Evidently, Trevor Fox went where the money was. Why she'd thought she could be in love with him, she didn't know.

She stood on the porch, watching Tia pull bushes out from where they'd washed under the house. She knew she should help, but she was waiting for Trevor. She'd hoped he would follow her out of the bedroom and give her some sort of explanation for his behavior. That he hadn't come out, but was still with Jeff, only added to her anger.

Boy, had she misjudged him. Uncle Nicky's comment that Trevor Fox could be bought was the truth. Once again, she'd thought she knew someone, only to discover she didn't. She'd dated Phil for seven months and hadn't known what a callous, self-important cad he was, not until she needed him. Why did she think she could know Trevor after only two days?

Two days.

She couldn't believe it had been that short a time. The last two days seemed like a lifetime.

From behind her came a sharp command. "Get off the porch."

Jana bristled the moment she heard Trevor's voice. Slowly, she turned to face him, hoping her glare expressed her feelings. She didn't have a chance to voice them. Before she could say a word, he grabbed her by the shoulders and pulled her to him.

"What the—" she started, her body slamming into his.

He put a hand over her mouth, holding her close so she was shielded from view, then he nodded toward the houses to the right of the porch.

Men, women, and children were working outside their homes, hauling away the debris scattered over the island by the hurricane, but Trevor wasn't looking at them. His gaze went beyond the islanders, to an area between two houses. There, his back to them, stood a man.

His skin was tanned, but not the darker pigment of the others working around their homes, and his suit wasn't something one of the islanders would wear, not when cleaning up after a hurricane. Jana stared at him, understanding Trevor's actions. Slowly, the man turned their way.

"Is that Alvarez?" Trevor asked quietly, lifting his hand from her mouth but keeping them back and out of sight.

"No." But she recognized the man. "It's Nardo, one of his bodyguards."

"I don't think he saw you."

Jana leaned her head against Trevor's chest, her legs suddenly weak. In her anger, she'd forgotten to keep out of sight. Again she hadn't planned ahead, and Trevor had had to come to her rescue.

Through his shirt, she could feel as well as hear Trevor's heartbeat. She didn't want to be soothed by it, yet she was. She didn't want to feel warm and safe in his arms, yet there was no denying those feelings. She did love him, whether it was good or bad.

Nardo started walking away from them, and she felt Trevor's sigh. He kept watching until Nardo was out of sight, then he looked down at her. The tight line of his jaw signaled his irritation.

"What did you think you were doing?" he demanded. "Standing out there where you could be seen? You might as well wave a red flag and tell them your stepbrother is here."

"Maybe I wanted to be seen." She pushed herself out of his embrace. "It would be better than having you set Jeff free."

"Is that what you think I was doing?"

She looked back toward the bedroom. "Maybe not right now, but you're going to. Money does talk."

"And you think I'd go for the money."

She looked into his eyes and wished she knew what to think. "I want to believe you wouldn't cut a deal with him." With all her heart and soul she wanted to believe that. "I want to think you're honest and heroic, trustworthy and everything noble."

She felt the tears coming and blinked them back. "I used to think of my father in those terms. I wanted to grow up and marry someone just like him. And then I found out what he was really like."

"I'm not your father."

"I know. But I also know I don't seem to have very good judgment when it comes to men. In college the guy I was going with was expelled for cheating on an exam.

And look at Jeff. I never would have brought him into the bank, wouldn't have let him near my computer, if I'd thought he was a hacker who would take other people's money. I just don't know how to tell when someone's honest or not."

Trevor shook his head. "I think if you're going to question my honesty, you'd better look at your own."

His words cut deep. She knew he was right. She felt guilty enough about the lies she'd told him, about everything she'd done to him. "Okay, I've been using you, and I shouldn't have, and it's ridiculous for me to think you should be so noble, but I—"

He stopped her, pulling her close again. "Oh, Jana, it's not ridiculous to want to be able to trust someone. People have to be able to trust each other. So trust me. I am not going to set your stepbrother free. For one thing, I may be a sucker for a pretty face, but I'm not stupid enough to think I'd ever see any money once Jeff was safely off this island." Trevor laughed, the rumble traveling to her body. "Even if he did pay me off, he'd probably turn around and transfer the money out of my account before I had a chance to spend any of it. That man needs to be locked up."

She knew then why she loved him.

Trevor stood behind Charlie Walker and watched the old man turn the dial of his radio. Occasionally there was a sputter of static, but most of the time the only sound was the generator running outside the house that was providing the electricity for the radio.

Above them, the sun shone through the parts of the roof where the boards had been blown off. The floor beneath Trevor's feet was still wet from the rain that had fallen through those gaps in the roof.

Charlie's place was barely more than a one-room shack. Empty beer cans and radios of all types and sizes cluttered shelves and tabletops, and were stacked on each other on the floor. Some of the radios had been torn apart for parts. Others looked almost new. None were working.

"Once it dries out a little, this will work," Charlie said, looking up, his toothless smile hopeful.

"You keep trying, okay?" Trevor pushed the message he'd written closer to the old man.

"You said you'd be buying me some beer, man?"

Trevor nodded. "I'll stop by Cora's and have some sent over."

"I'd like some of that imported stuff, you know, man?"

"Then that's what you'll get." He again touched the paper by Charlie's arm. "You'll deliver this message?"

Charlie leaned closer to the paper. "I'm to say two planes are down, both here illegally, and the police are to get here quick. That right, man?"

"That's right."

Trevor left Charlie's place with little hope that even getting the police to the island would help. There was a good reason Jeff and the others had come here. In the Bahamas they were safe from extradition. If Jana wanted justice, they were going to have to find a way to get Jeff back to the United States.

He did stop at Cora's and paid for a six pack of U.S. domestic beer to be delivered to Charlie's place, but he asked her to wait an hour or two before delivering it. He wanted Charlie reasonably sober for as long as possible. After leaving Cora's, Trevor went down to the docks, keeping a sharp eye out for Alvarez and his men.

A dozen men or so were at the docks. A fishing boat that had been washed up onto the dock was being hoisted back into the water with winches and pulleys. He saw Lynden helping and walked toward him. From behind the boat, Joe appeared, then Wally and Turk. Trevor was glad to see that neither Hurricane Ned nor Alvarez had harmed any of his friends.

"How's it looking?" he asked as he neared Lynden.

"Looking good, man," Lynden answered, his gaze on the boat as they lifted it off the wooden dock, then eased it over the water. "As far as Joe can tell, no damage."

"That's Joe's boat?" Trevor, too, watched the fishing boat.

"His father's. One of these days be Joe's, if any fish left in these waters by then."

Trevor kept his gaze on the boat. It was bigger than some of the others. Sturdy. It might work.

Tia was in the kitchen muttering to herself when Trevor returned to the house. She looked his way and frowned. "Listen to him. If he keeps jerking on that bed like that, he gonna break it, man. I ready to hit him over head with frying pan."

"Just hang on a little longer. I think we're going to have him out of here soon. Where's Jana?"

Tia nodded to her left. "She says she gonna check out your father's house. Says her bag and book there."

Trevor looked in the direction of his father's house. "The idiot."

He worked his way toward the house by staying close to the other houses and keeping his eyes open for Alvarez and his men. He hoped Jana had been as careful. When he came into view of the yellow house, he stopped.

The damage was clearer in daylight. The veranda in front was missing, completely washed away, and the living room and part of the kitchen were gone. A few yellow boards lay scattered on the beach, like crumbs left by a giant monster that had come ashore and taken a bite.

A tree from the wooded side of the house had fallen, tearing through the roof and crushing interior walls. The back half of the house was leaning at a precarious angle, waiting for a strong wind to take it down. For Jana to have come here was truly foolish.

He saw the house move—just a quiver—and knew she was inside. Then he saw something else. Coming out of the woods, dragging the body of one of Jeff's cohorts between them, were Alvarez and his two men.

They were heading straight for the house.

THIRTEEN

The body was left on the sand, and one of the South Americans entered the slanting yellow house. Trevor started in that direction, unsure what to do. He didn't have a gun; he'd left Jana's with Tia. He was outnumbered and he didn't have a plan. Jana had a way of eliminating planning.

He saw the exterior of the house shake precariously, then heard a crashing sound. One of the walls fell inward, and Trevor stopped where he was, his stomach knotting with fear at the sound of a pained yell.

He cried out her name, and the two South Americans outside looked his way, then ran toward the fallen section. Trevor also headed in that direction, not wanting Alvarez or his men to get to her first. He was halfway to the house when he saw her.

Jana came running around the back side of what remained of the house, holding up her skirt with one hand and only briefly glancing back. Over her left shoulder was the strap of her oversized handbag, the leather purse slapping against her leg as she ran. Without hesitation, she headed straight for Lynden's house.

Trevor intercepted her between two houses, catching her arm and guiding her away from Lynden's. "I got it," she said breathlessly.

He glanced at her flushed face, her eyes bright with excitement, but he didn't pause to find out what "it" was. Not sure where to go, he led her to the church. There, he knew, they would be out of sight and still able to monitor what was happening in the village.

The church's massive wooden door hung at an angle, one of its hinges broken. Trevor helped Jana through the opening and led her away from the doorway. Part of the church's roof was missing, the building's limestone walls and crude wooden pews still wet from the rain that had blown in. Staying close to the walls, he inched his way to one of the window openings.

Glass had never covered the rectangular hole, and now its shutters were gone. Staying back so he couldn't be seen, he checked the area in his vision for any signs of Alvarez or his men. Only when he'd made a pass around the entire interior of the church, looking out each of its windows and assuring himself that they hadn't been seen or followed, did he return to Jana's side. She was grinning.

"Look." She held up a small spiral notebook. "It's everything we need."

She thumbed through a few pages, and he understood her pleasure. Bank names and numbers were listed on the pages, some with checkmarks beside them and some without.

Her smile faded a little. "My money's gone, though. The money I was going to pay you. I'm sorry."

Trevor remembered the wad of bills that she'd flipped through in his office. It was the promise of money that had gotten him into this mess, but the money didn't matter anymore. "Forget the money. You could have been killed back there. That place is ready to fall in on itself, and when I saw Alvarez and his men—"

"That place *did* fall in on itself," she said, grinning proudly. "I think I got one of them when I pulled that wall down."

"You did that? On purpose?"

"Let's say, I gave the wall a little help."

"Jana, it could have fallen on you."

She rose up on her toes and kissed his cheek. "But it didn't."

They stayed in the church until Trevor said he felt it was safe to leave. Jana appreciated the care he took getting them back to Lynden and Tia's. When she'd dashed out of the yellow house, all she'd wanted to do was get back to safety . . . and back to him. She hadn't thought of what might happen if Alvarez followed her. When Trevor caught her arm, she'd been more than willing to let him take over. This espionage business was not for her.

In the church, Trevor had said he'd found a way off the island. Jana knew now that they had to get off, and soon. By going back to the yellow house, she'd gotten Jeff's notebook, but she'd also let Alvarez know that she was still alive and in the village. He would be looking for her, and sooner or later he'd get to Lynden's.

Tia met them at the door. She looked in both directions, then scooted them inside, quickly closing the door behind them. "Lynden came just little while ago," she said. "You to be very careful. One of those men at docks, watching. Other two, he thinks, going house to house."

"Did he say if the boat was ready?" Trevor asked.

"He says you come when you can. They leave as soon as can."

Jana looked at Trevor. "How are we going to get Jeff on a boat without alerting Alvarez and his men?"

His gaze scanned her body, and he smiled.

The docks were busy, most of the men and some of the women working on cleaning up the mess Hurricane Ned had left. Jana saw Alvarez's man the moment they came into view of the docks. It was Carlos. He'd come to the bank with Alvarez several times, but he'd always stood back from her desk, his dark eyes scanning the room and anyone who happened to step inside. Today he was looking for them, his gaze darting from the face of one islander to another. Jana looked away.

For the last hour, Tia had used her artistic talents to disguise them. Carlos was looking for a white woman— for two or three whites. He would see none today.

The dye Tia had used to darken their skin was one she used on the batiks she created and sold. The ingredients were natural, she'd said, and in time would go away. At first, Jana had had her doubts, but once the juicy mixture was rubbed onto her body, she began to believe they might be able to pull it off. In more ways than one, she was not the same person who'd come to the island.

The clothes they were wearing helped. Trevor had on a baggy shirt and pants, not Lynden's but from someone much heavier than Trevor. The outfit hung loosely on his muscular body and resembled the clothes worn by half the islanders. His feet were also bare—a common practice, it seemed, on this island—and a floppy brown hat covered his blond hair and most of his face. Tia had used another mixture of dyes to darken the hairs of his scruffy beard, and with all his exposed skin now a shade of cocoa brown, Jana barely recognized him.

She hadn't recognized herself in the mirror. In addition to the long, wraparound skirt and cotton blouse Tia had loaned her earlier, Tia had wrapped a bright red turban of cloth around Jana's hair, completely covering its lighter color and straighter texture. Jana knew, to the unknowing, she could pass as Tia's sister, but she feared that Carlos would notice she was different, might remember her from the bank. One look at her eyes would definitely give her away. As they came nearer to him, she kept her gaze directed to the ground.

She smiled when she realized he had his right arm in a sling. From the yell she'd heard before escaping from the yellow house, she'd been sure she'd gotten one of them when she pulled the wall down. Now she knew which one.

"*Alto!*" Carlos ordered, stepping into their path, the

rifle in his left hand held in military fashion. "What you have in there?"

A shard of cold dread ran down Jana's spine as Carlos pointed at the massive rattan basket attached to the thick ropes the three of them were pulling on. Tia answered for them. "Fixen's, man." She nodded toward the workers on the dock. "We have fishin' nets here for them. No holes like ones caught in storm. New cables." She held her rope toward him. "You wanna help pull, man?"

"No, I don't want to help." Carlos glared at her and walked over to the side of the basket. "Open it."

Jana held her breath and kept staring at the ground. Tia uttered a sound of disgust loud enough for Carlos to hear and mumbled about people being as bad as hurricanes as she lifted the lid to the basket.

Jana hoped her stepbrother was smart enough to lie still under those nets, and hoped that Carlos didn't go poking around too much. She also hoped the man didn't question why Trevor wasn't saying anything. Afraid to look away from the stones at her feet, all Jana could do was listen and pray.

"Okay," Carlos finally said, his own voice laced with irritation. "Get this basket out of here."

"Sure, man," Tia said, returning to her rope and picking it up. "We just doing our job, you know what I mean, man?"

"Get out of here," Carlos repeated, and Jana was glad when Tia nodded a signal to start pulling.

Every step of the way to the boat, Jana felt Carlos's eyes on her back. She kept waiting for him to put two and two together and again call out *Alto*. Or to simply shoot them in the back.

Wally came over and took her rope from her, another man from the village took Tia's rope, and a third pushed the basket from behind, guiding it toward the loading plank. Standing back, Jana watched as the men lifted the basket onto the plank that spanned the water between the boat and the dock.

If the sea had been calm, the loading would have been an easy task, but the water was still choppy, and halfway up the plank the basket tilted precariously over the side. Trevor grabbed for it, knocking his hat off as he did, his sandy blond hair highlighted by the sunlight. Jana turned to see what Carlos was doing, fear coursing through her veins and her legs turning to lead.

He was lighting a cigarette, his rifle leaning against one of the pylons as he managed the lighter with his left hand.

By the time Jana looked back at Trevor, another hat covered his hair, donated by one of the islanders, and the basket was safely on the boat.

"You come, yes?" Gaddy said, taking her arm and guiding her toward the plank. He glanced back at Carlos, then urged her to hurry.

Trevor took over as soon as she reached the end of the plank. He helped her onto the rocking boat, and nodded a thank you to Gaddy. Always aware of Carlos, they hurried to get the basket below deck. Only then did they pull the nets off Jeff and help him out.

They couldn't leave right away. The basket was emptied and a few torn nets were placed into it, just in case Carlos stopped them again and checked. Joe tried the engine several times before it caught, its steady putt interrupted occasionally by a missed beat. Lynden lifted his eyebrows in question, and Tia crossed her fingers, then gave Trevor a hug and a kiss.

Turning to Jana, she said, "You come back, okay. Better time." She nodded at Trevor. "Bring him back. We miss the sly fox."

"Because when I'm around," Trevor said, "life is never dull." He gave Tia one last hug, then spoke to Lynden. "Be careful. Those men aren't going to like not finding us. Have Charlie keep calling for help. Tell the authorities you found cocaine on the South American's plane. That ought to get them here a little quicker."

Lynden nodded. "You take care, man."

Lynden, Tia, and another woman, close to Jana's size, who'd taken the red cloth from Jana's head and wrapped it around her own, pulled the basket back off the dock and into the village. Carlos watched them pass but didn't stop them. A half hour later, the fishing boat pulled away from the dock.

Jana stayed below and made sure her stepbrother was comfortable, but she refused to loosen the ropes binding his hands, and when he began cursing her, she used Tia's trick and covered his mouth with tape.

Joe and his father offered her food, but she politely refused. The flies she'd seen on it were enough to turn her stomach. She was also discovering she wasn't much of a sailor. The more the boat pitched, the more her stomach threatened to have her leaning over the side. Exhausted, she lay on a pile of nets, not the least bit bothered by the hard knots under her.

She wasn't sure when she fell asleep or how long she slept, but it was dark by the time she went up on deck. The water was calmer, the putt-putt of the boat's engine a steady rhythm accompanied by the sound of waves lapping against the sides of the boat. Above her, the sky was nearly clear, only a few clouds here and there. The blue-black panorama was sprinkled with stars, while the light from the moon reflected off the water and was enough for her to see Trevor. He was leaning against the railing near the stern of the boat, and she walked over to him.

He glanced at her, then slipped an arm around her shoulders. He didn't speak, and she was content with the silence. There was so much she wanted to say, but she didn't know the right words. In three days they'd gone from complete strangers to enemies to intimate lovers. They'd faced dangers together, had learned to depend on each other, and had found love.

At least she knew she loved him. How he felt about her was the unknown, and how he would feel in a few days was the bigger question. Once they returned to the States, her future would be in the hands of others. She had her stepbrother and she had the notebook with the account numbers, but she didn't have any guarantee the authorities would believe her innocence. Asking for Trevor's love would be unfair. What she needed to do was set him free.

"I never thought we'd get off that island," she said.

He hugged her closer. "But we did."

"I can't wait to get back to Michigan." She pulled slightly away from him, her gaze on the water. "I want to forget everything that's happened these last two months."

"Everything?"

She heard the hesitancy in his voice, and it hurt her, but she knew she had to cut the ties. It would be the first unselfish thing she'd done for him. She glanced at him, then looked back at the water. "Everything."

The silence between them was no longer comfortable. She said nothing, letting him absorb her words and meaning. After a time, he spoke. "So what are you saying? Thanks, it's been fun, but it's over now?"

She'd been playacting when she first met him. She called on those skills again and lifted her eyebrows in question when she turned to him. "I really didn't expect to get off the island. When you and I . . . Well, what I mean is—" She wrinkled her nose and shook her head before looking away. "I guess what I'm trying to say is, Jeff was right. Under other circumstances, I wouldn't have looked at you twice. I'm really sorry your plane got wrecked and that they took the money I was going to pay you, but let's be honest with each other. You and I are as opposite as night and day. To think anything long term might develop, well—"

He didn't wait for her to finish. "You sound like Lila. The one who got me in trouble while I was in the marines."

Jana looked at him, the pain on his face tearing at her insides. She knew she had to get away before she confessed that she didn't mean a word of what she was saying. Stepping away, she started for the cabin.

"That's it?" he called after her.

She paused and looked back. "What more could there be?"

"Good question."

The sun was beating down on the small fishing boat when the sleek Coast Guard cutter came into view. Trevor watched it near and knew the saga had come to an end. They'd entered United States territorial waters. Joe and his father would be detained for a while, then sent back to Conch Island. Jeff and Jana would be turned over to the authorities—probably the FBI—and they would be gone. As for him?

He didn't know what would happen to him, and he wasn't sure he cared.

He watched Jana lean against the railing. The breeze blowing across the water feathered her hair back from her face. Her skin was still stained a cocoa brown, and she was still wearing Tia's skirt and blouse. He would remember her like this. And he would remember her naked beneath him, breathing his name as she reached her climax. He would remember so many things.

Mostly, he would remember he loved her.

FOURTEEN

"You can take your damned insurance policy and shove it!" Trevor shouted into the telephone, then slammed down the receiver. Leaning over the counter, he cradled his head in his hands and closed his eyes.

If things could get any worse, he didn't know how. He owed the bank more than he could ever come up with, especially since the plane he was in hock for was standing on its nose roughly three hundred miles from where he was and sure wasn't going to be earning him any income in the foreseeable future. Why he'd been paying that horrendous insurance premium, he didn't know. They certainly weren't going to give him any of the money back.

The way things were going, the airport manager would be in there next, handing him an eviction notice. Which really wouldn't matter since it was hard to run a charter service without a plane.

He heard the outside door open and slowly lifted his

head, half expecting to see the airport manager. The man who stepped into Fox's Charters' office, however, was not the airport manager, and Trevor knew that things had just gotten worse.

"Nicholas Scarlotti."

Scarlotti bowed his head slightly, just a hint of a smile touching his lips. "I see the young Fox has not forgotten me."

"You do make an impression."

Even in his seventies, Scarlotti was an impressive sight. Impeccably dressed in a navy blue pin-striped suit, his gray hair still thick, and his dark brown eyes as piercing as ever, he glanced around the reception area. His gaze stopped on a poster showing Trevor standing beside his Navajo and advertising the charter service. "You always did want to fly."

"It came from watching all those planes fly in and out of Conch Island when I was a teenager. Some nights, that airstrip was as busy as JFK."

"It served its purpose." Scarlotti walked closer to the counter. "I came to thank you. You also served my purpose. Served it well."

Trevor shook his head. "They still arrested her."

"She's a key witness. As soon as the trial is over, her life will be her own again."

"She testified on my behalf, you know." Trevor hadn't expected it. "Not in person, but she gave a deposition to the FBI, who in turn presented it at my hearing. She took all the blame, confessed to hijacking my plane and forcing me to fly below radar and into international waters without filing a flight plan."

"She wasn't like the other, was she?"

"No, she wasn't." He'd come to that conclusion while they were on the island, but he'd had his doubts after what she'd said on the boat.

"Our Jana is different."

"Definitely different." She was unpredictable, daring, and the woman he loved, like it or not. Except it had been three months since the Coast Guard had boarded that fishing boat. Three months since he'd talked to her. "Is she all right?"

"As well as can be expected."

One thing had been bothering him, one thing he had to know. "She's not pregnant, is she?"

Bushy gray eyebrows rose slightly. "How would you feel if she was?"

Trevor had wondered about that, his emotions ranging from praying that she wasn't pregnant to hoping she was. "Under the circumstances, it wouldn't be the best thing."

"But if she was?"

"I would ask her to marry me."

"Good." Scarlotti nodded, then shook his head. "But no, she is not pregnant. I understand she doesn't eat and is thin as a rail. If her father could see her now, bless his soul, he would say I wasn't taking good care of her."

"And is that your role? Are you her guardian? Her godfather?" Trevor had always felt Scarlotti fit the Godfather image. He was the essence of a mob boss; dapper, smooth, and deadly.

Scarlotti again shook his head. "I watch over Jana because her father was a good friend of mine. Your father was also a good friend of mine." He smiled. "It seemed appropriate to bring the two of you together."

"If you think I'm going to thank you, forget it." How could he thank him? Scarlotti had brought them together only long enough for Trevor to lose his heart. Now he had nothing. "I never did understand your relationship with my father."

"What is there to understand? We were two men separated from the world we knew. Isolated on that island. I liked him because he found beauty where it wasn't. He had a good mind."

"Most people called him crazy."

"Crazy like a fox."

"Yeah." Trevor smiled, remembering his father. He missed the man.

"He did what he wanted. Lived the way he wanted. Was he crazy or are we?"

Trevor knew he was going out of his mind. Looking down at the counter, he shook his head and decided he was the crazy one.

"Do you love her?"

He looked back up. Was he that transparent?

"Yes or no," Scarlotti pushed.

"I said I'd marry her, didn't I?"

"You said you'd marry her if she was pregnant. That's not what I asked. Do you love her?"

Trevor responded slowly. "The answer is, it doesn't matter how I feel. She walked away from me, said we have nothing in common. I've called her. She won't take my calls. I've written. No response."

"She doesn't feel her life is hers right now."

"Maybe she's not the only one."

Scarlotti gave him an assessing glance. Trevor knew he looked like hell. Getting dressed to meet the public didn't seem important when your heart was breaking and your plane was a crumpled pile of metal.

"I liked you as a boy," Scarlotti said. "You were curious. Adventurous."

"And curiosity almost killed the Fox."

"If you had opened your mouth, yes."

It didn't ease the tension running through him to hear that he'd been right, that if he'd told about the cocaine stored in that cave he would have met with an untimely death. As if any death was timely. "You nearly ruined that island."

"I left, didn't I?"

"Not before you set fire to your house and nearly burned down the village."

Scarlotti merely shrugged. "Some things are necessary, but that's what I like about you. You care. When she came to me, looking for help, I knew you would protect her."

Trevor shook his head, smiling as he thought of Jana. "She didn't have a very good plan. She has a way of jumping into things without thinking them completely through."

"She's half Italian. Italians are impetuous, don't you know that?" He laughed, and Trevor had a feeling Nicholas Scarlotti had never done an impetuous thing in his life.

As quickly as the laughter came, it was gone, and Scarlotti grew serious again. "You are right about her.

She never should have let her stepbrother near her computer, shouldn't have trusted him. Now she's leery of her judgment, afraid to believe in her emotions. Afraid to believe in your emotions. I think she has this idea that now that you're back in the 'real' world, as she puts it, you won't feel the same way as you did on the island. What you experienced together, she says, was 'unreal.' At least that's what she told her lawyer. I haven't talked to her. I don't talk to her." The smile returned, pensive but warm. "Like her mother, she wants to forget her past. It took a lot for her to come to me for help. I would have helped her more if I could have. I did the next best thing I could."

"You sent her to me." Trevor understood.

"I've kept track of you. You don't always show good judgment." There was almost a twinkle in his eyes. "Especially when it comes to women, but your heart is good. I knew you would take care of her. They got Alvarez, you know."

"So I heard."

"I wouldn't want to be in his shoes. He was laundering money. His superiors are not happy that that money is now in the hands of the FBI. I think Senor Alvarez may not be seeing another spring."

"You guys play rough." Trevor shook his head. "I don't want any part of this, Scarlotti."

"Neither does Jana. If she comes to you, you will take care of her?"

"If she comes to me."

"I ask you again. Do you love her?"

There seemed no point in denying it. "Yeah, I love her."

"Good." Scarlotti nodded, then reached into his inside coat pocket and pulled out a thick envelope. "She promised you a payment if you flew her where she wanted to go. I understand the money was lost. I am paying you. But she is not to know. You tell her the insurance money covered everything. Understand?"

Trevor took the envelope Scarlotti handed him. Opening it, he thumbed through the bills. There were far more than what Jana had promised, far more than Trevor could imagine. "I can't take this," he said, looking up.

Scarlotti was already back by the door. "Consider it a wedding gift."

"And what if she doesn't want to marry me?"

"There's a reason she's not eating, and I don't think it's because she's worried about this trial. I think it's because she misses someone, someone very special. Don't give up on her."

Trevor watched Nicholas Scarlotti leave the building and walk over to a sleek white BMW. A man wearing a gray suit opened the rear car door for him, and Scarlotti slid into the backseat. He glanced toward the building and gave the slightest of nods, then the car door was closed, the driver got back in, and Nicholas Scarlotti was gone.

The moment Jana arrived at Fox's Charters, she noticed differences from her last visit. Trevor's reception area now had furniture—two chairs and a bench—and a receptionist. The name plaque on the counter said Debra Wainwright.

Debra looked around forty, had blond hair that probably wasn't natural, and a dark tan. She was attractive, but not especially sexy or beautiful, and Jana found that a relief. She was willing to admit she could be jealous.

Debra's greeting when Jana stepped through the door was warm and cheerful. "Hi. Can I help you?"

"I'm looking for Trevor Fox." Jana walked up to the counter, trying to see into the office behind Debra. It had been so long since she'd last seen Trevor. Her stomach was in knots, her heart beating a mile a minute.

"I'm afraid he's out right now."

"Out?" The knots in her stomach did a twist, disappointment cutting through her. It had taken her all day to get up the nerve to come to the airport. She'd assumed he would be there.

"He's with a charter. May I help you?" Debra asked, still smiling. "Were you looking for a flying lesson or did you want to charter a trip?"

"I, ah . . . I want to charter a trip. Maybe." She needed to know how Trevor felt first. "I—I really need to talk to him, personally."

Debra glanced at the clock on the wall. It was nearly five. "He'll be here around six if you want to come back." Then she nodded toward the chairs. "Or you could wait."

Jana wasn't sure she'd find the nerve to come back. "I'll wait."

At five o'clock, Debra left, first asking Jana if there

was anything she needed. A dose of courage was the only thing that came to Jana's mind, so she shook her head no. At six o'clock, she wished she had that dose of courage, wished she knew if those days on the island still meant something to Trevor.

Planes had been flying in and out of the airport since she'd arrived, but when a twin engine taxied to a spot not far from the office, she knew it had to be Trevor's. It looked like the one he'd flown to Conch Island, yet it was different. Newer. Nicer.

The plane came to a complete stop and the steps went down, and the knots returned to her stomach. The moment she saw Trevor's legs on the steps, she stood, wanting a closer view.

He looked good. Different from the last time she'd seen him, but then the tan chinos and white shirt he was wearing hadn't been through a hurricane. And the scruffy beard she remembered from their last day together was gone, his face clean shaven. His skin was tanned, but not a shade of cocoa. Neither was hers. The dye Tia had used had finally worn off.

The setting sun glinted off his sandy blond hair, and aviator sunglasses shielded his eyes. He turned back toward the plane and helped a gray-haired woman out, then a nearly bald man. All three stood beside the plane for a minute, talking. Jana couldn't hear what they were saying, but she could tell from their body language that the couple was satisfied with their flight.

They started toward the office, and Jana turned toward the side door, waiting for the three of them to come through it—waiting for Trevor's reaction.

She knew how she was reacting. Simply seeing him had her legs shaking and her heart racing. For the last seven months, she'd wondered how it would be when she saw him again. Sometimes the days they'd spent together seemed like a dream, part nightmare and part bliss. Alone and wanting him, she would wonder if she'd made him into more than he really was. Seeing him again, she knew he was everything she'd remembered.

He held the door open for the couple and they entered first. They smiled politely when they saw her and proceeded on to the counter. Trevor was watching them when he stepped into the room. He didn't notice her right away.

And then he did.

He stopped midstep and stared at her.

He didn't say her name aloud, but she saw him form the word. He pulled off his sunglasses, as if not believing his eyes.

"I think we'd like to go up again on the fifteenth," the balding man said, checking a day planner his wife had taken out of her purse.

Trevor's gaze snapped to the man, then back to Jana. He pointed at her. "Give me a minute," he said, then walked to the back of his counter and opened a scheduling book. "The fifteenth would work out fine." He picked up a pen. "Same time or earlier?"

The man looked at his wife, then shrugged. "Same time, I guess."

"Okay." Trevor wrote in the book. "You're down for the fifteenth. Give me a call if anything comes up and you can't make it."

He smiled warmly at the couple, but Jana caught him glancing her way. The pair said their good-byes and promised they'd be back, then they were gone and a hush fell over Trevor's office.

He stared at her, but didn't say anything. She licked her lips, not sure what to say herself. A slight smile touched his lips, and he finally spoke. "Hi."

It was so simple, and not what she'd expected. She managed a smile of her own. "Hi, to you."

He didn't move. "I didn't expect to see you again."

"I wasn't sure if I should come." But in the end, she'd realized she had to come.

"I called you. Several times. You never returned my calls."

"I—I needed time. I needed to get some things behind me."

"I followed the trial. That is, what little they printed in the paper down here and what I caught on the evening news."

"It was quite an experience. Something I don't want to go through again." And she didn't want to talk about it, not now. She'd come to see him, see how he felt . . . if he cared. He looked uncomfortable.

"I want to thank you for that deposition you gave," he said. "I thought I'd had it for sure, then that FBI agent showed up and bam, everything changed. I became a hero."

"It was the least I could do, and you were a hero." She glanced around his office. "I see a lot of things have changed. New plane. Furniture. Receptionist. Your insurance company did pay?"

"I received a very nice payment."

"I'm glad. I worried about that. I was afraid they wouldn't under the circumstances. I asked the bank to give you the reward they were offering. Did they?"

He shook his head.

"They should have. We never would have gotten Jeff back or the notebook with the account numbers without you."

"You played a part in all that. Just about got yourself killed, in fact, getting that notebook." He walked around the counter and across the room, stopping when he was only inches away from her.

She caught herself holding her breath as he neared and forced herself to exhale. His gaze drifted down over her short-sleeved white cotton blouse and dark blue miniskirt, then dropped to the leather sandals on her feet. This time she hadn't dressed as provocatively as the first time they'd met, but she'd chosen her outfit carefully, wanting to look nice for him.

He reached out and touched her bare arm, and she did hold her breath. Staring into eyes as blue as the sea, she waited.

"You are thin," he said, his fingertip trailing over her skin and sending a shiver down her spine. Then he combed his fingers through her hair, letting it fall back to her shoulders. He was devouring her with his eyes, and she knew she'd made the right decision in coming.

She wasn't sure what she would have done if his reception had been cold or angry. Once again, she hadn't planned that far ahead. She'd come because she had to. That was all she knew.

"Why didn't you answer my calls? My letters?"

She heard the hurt. "I didn't know what to say to you."

"Hello. How are you, are always good for starters." She tried to smile. "It wouldn't have been enough."

"I could have come up. Been with you."

She shook her head. "I didn't know how it was going to turn out, and I didn't want you implicated in any way." She put a hand on his arm, feeling the strength in his sinewy muscles. "I dragged you into this. You never should have been involved."

"You didn't drag me into it. Nicholas Scarlotti involved me." Trevor smiled. "Or maybe it was fate."

"I kept your letters." She patted the leather handbag by her side. Although it was water stained and scuffed, she carried it with her as a reminder of her days with Trevor. "They're in here."

"Along with a handgun?" He cocked his head, grinning at her.

"Not this time."

"If you read the letters I sent, you knew how I felt."

"Let's see. In those letters you said you hoped everything was going well, that you'd heard from Tia and the village was gradually getting back to normal, that all of the boats were back in the water and most of the debris left from Hurricane Ned had been cleared away, including what was left of your father's house. You wrote about the weather here in Florida, about your mother visiting you, and about your hearing. You didn't say anything about how you felt."

He grimaced. "Well, you should have known. I

wrote, didn't I? Besides, I wasn't going to spill my guts when I wasn't sure you even wanted to hear from me. On the boat you said I wasn't your type."

"You're not." Looking at him, she shook her head. "Trevor, I had to say what I said, that night on the fishing boat. I could have ended up in jail. They might have pressed charges, claimed I was in on the robbery with Jeff and simply got cold feet. I could have gotten ten to twenty years in prison. What were you going to do, wait around for me?"

"Maybe."

She grinned. "You're crazy, you know."

"You have a way of driving a person crazy."

"How would you like to fly me to the Bahamas?"

He lifted his eyebrows. "Any particular island?"

"I have one in mind. It's not a very big island. Doesn't even have a real airport, just an airstrip." She ran a fingertip over his forearm. "It does have a couple of interesting caves."

"Oh yeah? So you want to go to the Bahamas to explore caves?"

"I want to explore something."

He cradled her face in his hands, tilting it up. "Have you thought this through?"

"No. I figured we could go there and—" She shrugged and smiled. "See what happens."

"You know what?" He drew her closer. "I have an apartment not too far from here. It even has a bed. What do you say we go there and see what happens?"

"I'm not sure I'd know how to act with you in a bed."

"I think you'll know." He hugged her and brushed a kiss over her forehead. "We are different."

She knew he wasn't talking about their physical differences. "We've got a lot to learn about each other.

"I'm not interested in climbing any corporate ladder, but I do believe in fidelity and family and long-term commitments."

"And you love to fly."

He stepped back, his gaze concerned. "I know your father's death and lifestyle had a big impact on you, Jana. Really, I never have been involved in drugs. And if you're worried about my flying . . . Well, flying really is safe, safer than driving a car, but if—"

She stopped him. "Once I got to know you, I knew you hadn't been involved with drugs. It's just not your nature. And I don't want you to give up flying. In fact, maybe you can give me flying lessons." She grinned. "So next time I decide to hijack a plane, I'll really know what I'm doing."

"I've missed you, honey," he murmured, gathering her back in his arms. And as Trevor's lips touched hers, Jana knew she was going to have to thank Nicholas Scarlotti some day. Maybe when she sent him a wedding announcement.

THE EDITORS' CORNER

As the year draws to a close, we're delighted to bring you some Christmas cheer to warm and gladden your hearts. December's LOVESWEPTs will put a smile on your face and love on your mind, and when you turn that last page, you'll sigh longingly and maybe even wipe a few stray tears off your cheeks.

Rachel Lawrence and Sam Wyatt are setting off **FIREWORKS** in LOVESWEPT #862 by rising star RaeAnne Thayne. The last time Rachel left Whiskey Creek, she swore she'd never return. The only two people in the world who can force her to break her vow are her nephews. The problem is, Rachel and their father, Sam, can't stand each other. Now that Rachel's back in town, the sparks are flying. Sam can't understand why Rachel would take such a vested interest in the welfare of his sons—he just wants her to leave before he acts on the desire he feels for her. Rachel fears giving in to feelings for Sam she's harbored in her heart, harbored even before she lost her young husband in a brushfire. But when another brushfire threatens to claim the family ranch, will she forgive Sam for choosing duty over love? RaeAnne Thayne's tale sizzles with passion and is sure to keep you warm on even the coldest winter night!

In LOVESWEPT #863, Laura Taylor delivers **THE CHRISTMAS GIFT.** Former attorney Jack Howell thought his toughest cases were behind him, but when he returns to Kentucky to explore his new-found roots, he faces his most baffling case of all—an infant boy abandoned on his doorstep. Interior decorator Chloe McNeil's temper starts to simmer when Jack doesn't keep their appointment to discuss his new home. Maybe she's misjudged this man who so easily found a way into her heart. But when she drops by to give him a piece of her mind, she finds him knee-deep in diapers and formula. As Jack and Chloe care for the baby and try to keep Social Services from taking him away, will they discover that cherishing this child together is just the healing magic they need? Well-loved author Laura Taylor unites two wounded spirits during the season of Christmas harmony.

Remember Candy Johnson, Jen Casey's best friend in FOR LOVE OR MONEY, LOVESWEPT #849? Well, she's back with a hunk of her own in Kathy DiSanto's **HUNTER IN DISGUISE,** LOVE-SWEPT #864. Candy is sure there's more to George Price than his chunky glasses and ever-present pocket protector. For example, a chest and tush of Greek-god standards. And why would a gym teacher take out the soccer balls for the girls vs. guys volleyball match? And let's not forget about his penchant for B 'n' E (break-ing and entering, that is). In the meantime, George has a problem all his own—trying to distract armchair detective Candy long enough to get his job done. George's less-than-debonair attributes prove to be easy enough to ignore as Candy gets to know the man beneath the look. Kathy DiSanto spins a breathless tale that's part wicked romp, part sexy suspense, and all pure pleasure!

Please welcome newcomer Catherine Mulvany to our Loveswept family as she presents **UPON A MIDNIGHT CLEAR**, LOVESWEPT #865. Alexandra Roundtree's obituary clearly stated she was no longer one of Brunswick, Oregon's, living citizens, but private investigator Dixon Yano is disabused of that notion when she comes walking into his agency in full disguise. Alex pleads with Dixon to help her find her would-be murderer, and after shots are fired through his window, Dixon decides to be her bodyguard. Soon, Dixon and Alex are forced into close quarters and intimate encounters. Even after her last romantic fiasco, Alex finds herself trusting in the man who has become her swashbuckling hero and lifesaver. Will Dixon cross the line between business and pleasure if it means risking his lady's life? Catherine Mulvany's first novel mixes up an explosively sensual cocktail that will touch and tantalize the soul!

Happy reading!

With warmest wishes,

Susann Brailey

Joy Abella

Susann Brailey   Joy Abella
Senior Editor   Administrative Editor

P.S. Look for these Bantam women's fiction titles coming in December! *New York Times* bestseller Iris Johansen is back with **LONG AFTER MIDNIGHT,** now available in paperback. Research scientist Kate Denham mistakenly believes she's finally carved out a secure life for herself and her son, only to be thrown suddenly into a nightmare world where danger is all around and trusting a handsome stranger is the only way to survive. Hailed as "a queen of erotic, exciting romance," Susan Johnson gives us **TABOO.** Andre Duras and Teo Korsakova are thrown together during the chaotic times of the Napoleonic Wars, igniting a glorious passion even as conflicting loyalties threaten to tear them apart. And finally, a charmer from the gifted Michelle Martin—**STOLEN MOMENTS**—a stylish contemporary romance about the man hired to track down a beautiful young pop singer who is tired of fame and has decided to explore Manhattan incognito. And immediately following this page, preview the Bantam women's fiction titles on sale in October!

For current information on Bantam's women's fiction, visit our Web site, *Isn't It Romantic*, at the following address: **http://www.bdd.com/romance**

Don't miss these extraordinary books
by your favorite Bantam authors!

On sale in October:

FINDING LAURA
by Kay Hooper

HAWK O'TOOLE'S HOSTAGE
by Sandra Brown

IT HAPPENED ONE NIGHT
by Leslie LaFoy

POWER AND MONEY ARE
NO PROTECTION FROM FATE—
OR MURDER. . . .

FINDING LAURA
by Kay Hooper

Over the years, the wealthy, aloof Kilbourne family has suffered a number of suspicious deaths. Now the charming, seductive Peter Kilbourne has been found stabbed to death in a seedy motel room. And for Laura Sutherland, a struggling artist, nothing will ever be the same. Because she was one of the last people to see him alive—and one of the first to be suspected of his murder.

Now, determined to clear her name and uncover the truth about the murder—and the antique mirror that had recently brought Peter into her life—Laura will breach the iron gates of the Kilbourne estate . . . only to find that every Kilbourne, from the enigmatic Daniel to the steely matriarch Amelia to Peter's disfigured widow, Kerry, has something to hide. But which one of them looks in the mirror and sees the reflection of a killer? And which one will choose Laura to be the next to die?

"Miss Sutherland? I'm Peter Kilbourne."

A voice to break hearts.

Laura gathered her wits and stepped back, opening the door wider to admit him. "Come in." She thought he was about her own age, maybe a year or two older.

He came into the apartment and into the living room, taking in his surroundings quickly but thoroughly, and clearly taking note of the mirror on the coffee table. His gaze might have widened a bit when it fell on her collection of mirrors, but Laura couldn't be sure, and when he turned to face her, he was smiling with every ounce of his charm.

It was unsettling how instantly and powerfully she was affected by that magnetism. Laura had never considered herself vulnerable to charming men, but she knew without doubt that this one would be difficult to resist—whatever it was he wanted of her. Too uneasy to sit down or invite him to, Laura merely stood with one hand on the back of a chair and eyed him with what she hoped was a faint, polite smile.

If Peter Kilbourne thought she was being ungracious in not inviting him to sit down, he didn't show it. He gestured slightly toward the coffee table and said, "I see you've been hard at work, Miss Sutherland."

She managed a shrug. "It was badly tarnished. I wanted to get a better look at the pattern."

He nodded, his gaze tracking past her briefly to once again note the collection of mirrors near the hallway. "You have quite a collection. Have you . . . always collected mirrors?"

It struck her as an odd question somehow, perhaps because there was something hesitant in his tone, something a bit surprised in his eyes. But Laura replied truthfully despite another stab of uneasiness. "Since I was a child, actually. So you can see why I bought that one today at the auction."

"Yes." He slid his hands into the pockets of his dark slacks, sweeping open his suit jacket as he did so in a pose that might have been studied or merely relaxed. "Miss Sutherland—look, do you mind if I call you Laura?"

"No, of course not."

"Thank you," he nodded gravely, a faint glint of amusement in his eyes recognizing her reluctance. "I'm Peter."

She nodded in turn, but didn't speak.

"Laura, would you be interested in selling the mirror back to me? At a profit, naturally."

"I'm sorry." She was shaking her head even before he finished speaking. "I don't want to sell the mirror."

"I'll give you a hundred for it."

Laura blinked in surprise, but again shook her head. "I'm not interested in making money, Mr. Kilbourne—"

"Peter."

A little impatiently, she said, "All right—Peter. I don't want to sell the mirror. And I did buy it legitimately."

"No one's saying you didn't, Laura," he soothed. "And you aren't to blame for my mistake, certainly. Look, the truth is that the mirror shouldn't have been put up for auction. It's been in my family a long time, and we'd like to have it back. Five hundred."

Not a bad profit on a five-dollar purchase. She drew a breath and spoke slowly. "No. I'm sorry, I really am, but . . . I've been looking for this—for a mirror like this—for a long time. To add to my collection. I'm not interested in making money, so please don't bother to raise your offer. Even five thousand wouldn't make a difference."

His eyes were narrowed slightly, very intent on her face, and when he smiled suddenly it was with rueful certainty. "Yes, I can see that. You don't have to look so uneasy, Laura—I'm not going to wrest the thing away from you by force."

"I never thought you would," she murmured, lying.

He chuckled, a rich sound that stroked along her nerve endings like a caress. "No? I'm afraid I've made you nervous, and that was never my intention. Why don't I buy you dinner some night as an apology?"

This man is dangerous. "That isn't necessary," she said.

"I insist."

Laura looked at his incredibly handsome face, that charming smile, and drew yet another deep breath. "Will your wife be coming along?" she asked mildly.

"If she's in town, certainly." His eyes were guileless.

Very dangerous. Laura shook her head. "Thanks, but no apology is necessary. You offered a generous price for the mirror; I refused. That's all there is to it." She half turned and made a little gesture toward the door with one hand, unmistakably inviting him to leave.

Peter's beautiful mouth twisted a bit, but he obeyed the gesture and followed her to the door. When she opened it and stood back, he paused to reach into the inner pocket of his jacket and produced a business card. "Call me if you change your mind," he said. "About the mirror, I mean."

Or anything else, his smile said.

"I'll do that," she returned politely, accepting the card.

"It was nice meeting you, Laura."

"Thank you. Nice meeting you," she murmured.

He gave her a last flashing smile, lifted a hand slightly in a small salute, and left her apartment.

Laura closed the door and leaned back against it for a moment, relieved and yet still uneasy. She didn't know why Peter Kilbourne wanted the mirror back badly enough to pay hundreds of dollars for it, but every instinct told her the matter was far from settled.

She hadn't heard the last of him.

Her novels are sensual and moving, compelling and richly satisfying. That's why *New York Times* bestselling phenomenon **Sandra Brown** is one of America's best-loved romance writers. Now, the passionate struggle between a modern-day outlaw and his feisty, beautiful captive erupts in

HAWK O'TOOLE'S HOSTAGE

To Hawk O'Toole, she was a pawn in a desperate gamble to help his people. To Miranda Price, he was a stranger who'd done the unthinkable: kidnapped her and her young son off a train full of sight-seeing vacationers. Now, held hostage on a distant reservation for reasons she cannot at first fathom, Miranda finds herself battling a captor who is by turns harsh and tender, mysteriously aloof and dangerously seductive.

"You know me?" She tried not to reveal her anxiety through her voice.

"I know who you are."

"Then you have me at a distinct disadvantage."

"That's right. I do."

She had hoped to weasel out his name, but he lapsed into stoic silence as the horse carefully picked its way down the steep incline. As hazardous as the race up the mountainside had been, traveling down the other side was more so. Miranda expected the horse's forelegs to buckle at any second and pitch them forward. They wouldn't stop rolling until they hit bottom several miles below. She was afraid for

Scott. He was still crying, though not hysterically as before.

"That man my son is riding with, does he know how to ride well?"

"Ernie was practically born on a horse. He won't let anything happen to the boy. He's got several sons of his own."

"Then he must understand how I feel!" she cried.

When she reflexively laid her hand on his thigh, she inadvertently touched his holster. The pistol was within her grasp! All she had to do was play it cool. If she could catch him off guard, she had a chance of whipping the pistol out of the holster and turning it on him. She could stave off the others while holding their leader at gunpoint long enough for Scott to get on the horse with her. Surely she could find her way back to the train where law enforcement agencies must already be organizing search parties. Their trail wouldn't be difficult to follow, for no efforts had been taken to cover it. They could still be found well before dark.

But in the meantime, she had to convince the outlaw that she was resigned to her plight and acquiescent to his will. Gradually, so as not to appear obvious, she let her body become more pliant against his chest. She ceased trying to maintain space between her thighs and his. She no longer kept her hip muscles contracted, but let them go soft against his lap, which grew perceptibly tighter and harder with each rocking motion of the saddle.

Eventually her head dropped backward onto his shoulder, as though she had dozed off. She made certain he could see that her eyes were closed. She knew he was looking down at her because she could feel his breath on her face and the side of her neck. Taking a deep breath, she intentionally lifted her breasts high, until they strained against her lightweight summer blouse. When they settled, they settled heavily on the arm he still held across her midriff.

But she didn't dare move her hand, not until she thought the moment was right. By then her heart had begun to pound so hard she was afraid he might feel it against his arm. Sweat had moistened her palms. She hoped her hand wouldn't be too slippery to grab the butt of the pistol. To avoid that, she knew she must act without further delay.

In one motion, she sat up straight and reached for the pistol.

He reacted quicker.

His fingers closed around her wrist like a vise and prized her hand off the gun. She grunted in pain and gave an anguished cry of defeat and frustration.

"Mommy?" Scott shouted from up ahead. "Mommy, what's the matter?"

Her teeth were clenched against the pain the outlaw was inflicting on the fragile bones of her wrist, but she managed to choke out, "Nothing, darling. Nothing. I'm fine." Her captor's grip relaxed, and she called to Scott, "How are you?"

"I'm thirsty and I have to go to the bathroom."

"Tell him it's not much farther."

She repeated the dictated message to her son. For the time being Scott seemed satisfied. Her captor let the others go on ahead until the last horse was almost out of sight before he placed one hand beneath her jaw and jerked her head around to face him.

"If you want to handle something hard and deadly, Mrs. Price, I'll be glad to direct your hand to something just as steely and fully loaded as the pistol. But then you already know how hard it is, don't you?

You've been grinding your soft little tush against it for the last twenty minutes." His eyes darkened. "Don't underestimate me again."

The situation had taken on a surreal aspect.

That was dispelled the moment the man dismounted and pulled her down to stand beside him. After the lengthy horseback ride, her thighs quivered under the effort of supporting her. Her feet were numb. Before she regained feeling in them, Scott hurled his small body at her shins and closed his arms around her thighs, burying his face in her lap.

She dropped to her knees in front of him and embraced him tightly, letting tears of relief roll down her cheeks. They had come this far and had escaped serious injury. She was grateful for that much. After a lengthy bear hug, she held Scott away from her and examined him. He seemed none the worse for wear, except for his eyes, which were red and puffy from crying. She drew him to her chest again and hugged him hard.

Too soon, a long shadow fell across them. Miranda looked up. Their kidnapper had taken off the white duster, his gloves, his gun belt, and his hat. His straight hair was as inky black as the darkness surrounding them. The firelight cast wavering shadows across his face that blunted its sharp angles but made it appear more sinister.

That didn't deter Scott. Before Miranda realized what he was going to do, the child flung himself against the man. He kicked at the long shins with his tennis shoes and pounded the hard, lean thighs with his grubby fists.

"You hurt my mommy. I'm gonna beat you up. You're a bad man. I hate you. I'm gonna kill you. You leave my mommy alone."

His high, piping voice filled the still night air. Miranda reached out to pull Scott back, but the man held up his hand to forestall her. He endured Scott's ineffectual attack until the child's strength had been spent and the boy collapsed into another torrent of tears.

The man took the boy's shoulders between his hands. "You are very brave."

His low, resonant voice calmed Scott instantly. With solemn, tear-flooded eyes, Scott gazed up at the man. "Huh?"

"You are very brave to go up against an enemy so much stronger than yourself." The others in the outlaw band had clustered around them, but the boy had the man's attention. He squatted down, putting himself on eye level with Scott. "It's also a fine thing for a man to defend his mother the way you just did." From a scabbard attached to his belt, he withdrew a knife. Its blade was short, but sufficient. Miranda drew in a quick breath. The man tossed the knife into the air. It turned end over end until he deftly caught it by the tip of the blade. He extended the ivory handle toward Scott.

"Keep this with you. If I ever hurt your mother, you can stab me in the heart with it."

Wearing a serious expression, Scott took the knife. Ordinarily, accepting a gift from a stranger would have warranted parental permission. Scott, his eyes fixed on the man before him, didn't even glance at Miranda. For the second time that afternoon, her son had obeyed this man without consulting her first. That, almost as much as their perilous situation, bothered her.

"Hmm. Can I go to the bathroom now?"

"There is no bathroom here. The best we can offer is the woods."

"That's okay. Sometimes Mommy lets me go outside if we're on picnics and stuff." He sounded agreeable enough, but he glanced warily at the wall of darkness beyond the glow of the campfire.

"Ernie will go with you," Hawk reassured him, pressing his shoulder as he stood up. "When you come back, he'll get you something to drink."

"Okay. I'm kinda hungry, too."

Ernie stepped forward and extended his hand to the boy, who took it without hesitation. They turned and, with the other men, headed toward the campfire. Miranda made to follow. The man named Hawk stepped in front of her and barred her path. "Where do you think you're going?"

"To keep an eye on my son."

"Your son will be fine without you."

"Get out of my way."

Instead, he clasped her upper arms and walked her backward until she came up against the rough bark of a pine tree. Hawk kept moving forward until his body was pinning hers against the tree trunk. The brilliant blue eyes moved over her face, down her neck, and across her chest.

"Your son seems to think you're worth fighting for." His head lowered, coming closer to hers. "Are you?"

IT HAPPENED ONE NIGHT
by Leslie LaFoy

*Alanna Chapman knows that no accountant worth her salt
would leave town during tax season, but now she has no
choice. To honor her aunt's final wishes, the Colorado CPA
has come to the mist-shrouded shores of Ireland, intending
to stay just long enough to accomplish her mission. But on
the mysterious grounds of Carraig Cor, something extraordinary happens: Alanna finds herself catapulted back to the
year 1803. Taken for a "seer" who can foretell Ireland's
future, she becomes the prisoner of a ruthless privateer . . . a dangerously attractive sea captain who has no
doubt that he can bend this modern temptress to his will, to
use her magic powers for his own ends. But when Alanna
crossed over to the nineteenth century, she didn't leave her
independent spirit behind. Now she's looking for a way to
escape the captain's irresistible embrace—and his enemy's
notice—before this perilous adventure costs her her
heart . . . and her life.*

Alanna raced to the door of the cabin, fighting back
panic and daring not a single look back. She knew
with absolute certainty that it wouldn't be long before
he staggered to his feet and came after her, that the
seconds between now and his vengeance were pre-

cious. The latch lifted and the door opened without resistance. Barefoot, with her hair streaming behind her, she fled down a dimly lit corridor toward a short flight of steep stairs. Hiking the gown above her knees, she clambered up the worn wooden steps, taking them two at a time. Her breath ragged and her heart pounding, she burst from the bowels of the ship onto the deck. Sliding to a sudden halt, Alanna glanced about the now clouded night, quickly noting the silent activity of shadowed male shapes and the world which lay beyond her floating prison. No light, of either man or heaven, sought to break the darkness. Her sight adjusted as she gazed to her left and out across the open sea. Turning to her right, she saw, beyond a wide expanse of green water, the rocky shoreline she had glimpsed from the window of Kiervan's cabin.

Ahead of her the ship narrowed to a long thick pole that stretched out over the sea. Alanna whirled about. The doorway from which she had emerged onto the deck sat in the center of a squat, flat-topped blockhouse. A few feet to her left another steep but short flight of stairs led upward. With relief, she noted that the structure didn't fill the entire width of the ship. On both sides, between it and the railings, a wide space permitted easy passage to the rear of the vessel. Pivoting to her right, Alanna dashed for the corner.

She was three-quarters of the way down the deck, with the unmistakable silhouette of a dinghy in sight, when a human shape stepped from around the corner and squarely into her path.

She stumbled to a halt. "Colleen, 'tis dangerous for ye to be topside, don't ye know? Where be Kiervan?"

Paddy. And he showed not the slightest signs of being inebriated. With a sigh of relief, Alanna moved toward him, keeping her voice low as she said, "He's a madman, Mr. O'Connell. He thinks it's 1803. He thinks he's some gun-running privateer."

"But for the first, 'tis all true, colleen. The lad's mind be far sounder than that of most men."

She froze and then managed to sputter, "It's 1997!"

He shook his head. " 'Twas before you climbed the Carraig Cor, to be sure. Least 'twas that time from which Maude promised to return to Erin. Now come along, colleen," he said, stepping forward and extending his hand, "an' I'll be a-seein' ye safely returned to Kiervan's cabin."

She stared at him, shaking her head and backing beyond his reach. "You're just as crazy as he is."

" 'Tis a long day ye've had, to be sure, an' 'twill be only a long rest which makes the edges of the world a wee bit smoother. 'Twill be easier for ye in the mornin'." He moved toward her again as he added, "Let's be about findin' Kiervan now."

Again Alanna shook her head. "I don't think so."

"Ye canna stay up here. My lads will do ye no harm, but Kiervan's have no respect for what ye are. And a British patrol could come upon us at any time. 'Tis not safe for ye to be remainin' topside."

She wasn't safe anywhere aboard this floating loony bin. Alanna glanced toward the rocky island in the distance. The impulse and the decision came in the same fraction of time. Without a word she spun about, grasped the railing, and vaulted over the side. In midair she righted herself and entered the water with knifelike precision.

On sale in November:

LONG AFTER MIDNIGHT
by *Iris Johansen*

TABOO
by *Susan Johnson*

STOLEN MOMENTS
by *Michelle Martin*